UNFINISHED WITCHNESS

HAUNTED HAVEN
BOOK ONE

ADA BELL

EMPRESS BOOKS

UNFINISHED WITCHNESS

Since inheriting her grandfather's hearth magic, Emma's chores have never been so much fun. Her house sparkles, dishes wash themselves, and her pancakes...Well, she's a witch, not a miracle worker. Emma's mansion would make a perfect bed-and-breakfast, if only she could deliver on that second "B". It's time to hire someone who can prepare a meal without burning the place down. Everything is going great until Emma's new chef turns up dead and police shut the venture down practically before it opens.

Determined to get back on track, Emma takes the investigation into her own hands. With magic, a talking cat, and ghostly grandfather, solving the murder should be a breeze, right? Wrong. Being incorporeal and tied to the mansion makes Grandpa Walter less than an ideal partner. The cat is as helpful as, well, your average house cat. And local police don't appreciate Emma's assistance one bit. Can she find the murderer or will she be forced to start over yet again?

PRAISE FOR ADA BELL

"*Mystic Pieces* is a charming, humorous, and original mystery that weaves a tale of murder and self-discovery with heart, family, and psychic visions."

— *READER'S FAVORITE*

"...I liked Aly as a main character and reading about her and her powers. I liked the side characters and how each had their own personality that made it easy to remember. All in all I really enjoyed this book and look forward to the next book in the series!"

— LOLA'S BOOK REVIEWS

"A cute and cozy introduction to the quirky and devoted characters, *Mystic Pieces* is the perfect first installment to the Shady Grove Psychic Mystery Series."

— LITERARY LIONESS

HAUNTED HAVEN

UNFINISHED WITCHNESS

The attached novel is a work of fiction. Any resemblance to actual persons, places, or events is merely a coincidence. But if you happen to be a witch with powers like Emma's, please reach out.

Empress Books

P.O. Box 1572

Clifton Park, NY 12065

To all of my Kickstarter backers,

Thank you for helping me bring this series to life.

"Once in New York, you are sure to be a great success. I know lots of people here who would give a hundred thousand dollars to have a grandfather, and much more than that to have a family ghost."

— OSCAR WILDE, *THE CANTERVILLE GHOST*

At the top of the driveway, I pulled my beaten old Toyota Corolla to a halt and gazed at the house in front of me. Wait. "House" was not the right word.

At the top of the driveway, I pulled my beaten old Toyota Corolla to a halt and gazed at the *giant freaking mansion* in front of me. The mansion that, unbelievably, now belonged to me. I'd seen the paperwork and everything. I was so afraid it would disappear, I'd stopped at a bank on the way here and gotten a safe deposit box for the documents. This gorgeous building definitely belonged to me.

Before someone could tell me there'd been a huge mistake, I'd driven over here with all of my meager worldly possessions in the back of my car, a black cat who'd adopted me, and the keys to this castle. Also bank records showing I could now access a mind-boggling amount of money at will. Which actually meant it might be time to consider replacing my beloved old rust bucket.

Just kidding.

Apparently, my prim and proper grandmother hadn't been as strait-laced as she had appeared because I'd learned recently that she'd had an affair with the prior owner of this house, Walter Sparrow. Their time together resulted in the birth of my mother. If that wasn't life-changing enough, Walter had been a witch, my grandmother was a witch, and so were their descendants. Namely me, since no one had seen my mother in about thirty years. If she had power, no one mentioned it.

My biological grandfather amassed a fortune over the years. When he died, he'd left the money with some extremely capable advisors. According to the accountant, I had almost twice as much money as when Walter died, and it had been a lot. Too bad I'd never get to thank him.

I'd already pinched myself about six hundred times in the past few hours, but just for good measure, I did it one more time. Nothing changed. This wasn't a dream.

"Did you want to go in, or should we stare at the house all day?" the cat asked. "If we wait long enough, those clouds should open up and get us nice and soaked."

That's right. My new cat talked. It unnerved me a bit at first, but I was getting used to it.

"Remind me again what you're doing here?" I asked.

"I'm your familiar," he said primly. "You need me."

"I'll be the judge of that," I said. "And why is a black cat named Pink?"

"My prior partner loved nineties music. And irony."

"He should have named you Alanis," I muttered.

"Don't start," he said.

"Hey, it's all good. I like the name. It suits you." I paused. "Wait. Wasn't your prior partner my grandfather?"

"No. When he died, I moved on for a bit. Now I'm back."

"Does every owner get to rename you?"

He rolled his eyes. Well, he raised his chin in what appeared to be the cat equivalent. "You're lucky I respond to 'Pink.' Do you intend to open the door?"

"I don't know. I don't need a familiar." The word felt weird in my mouth. Until recently, witches and animals that served as familiars were about as real as *Star Wars*. I pretended to rub my chin thoughtfully. "It might be nice to have a cat, though. I could get you one of those pink collars with a bell."

"Don't you dare," he said. "I'll turn you into a chicken before you can blink."

"Y—you can do that?"

"Let's hope you never find out."

There was no arguing with that, so I opened my car door and let us out.

The old Victorian-style mansion sat on several acres in the woods between the two small towns of Willow Falls and Shady Grove, New York. I'd never been to New York before a week ago, but my new home lay about twenty minutes north of Saratoga, about an hour and a half south of the Canadian border, and in a world where magic existed.

The main building was massive: three stories, plus a basement. Rumor said it housed forty-one rooms. Walter's lawyer said it was more like twenty, but still. My old apartment had three. I wondered how many bathrooms this place included. To the rear, I'd spotted several outbuildings when I drove up. An old barn could serve as a garage, but when I tugged at the door, it fell off the track. I'd have to fix it later. For now, the driveway worked fine.

To say the property had seen better days would be kind. Stone turrets that must have once been gorgeous lined the front door, but big patches of cement showed through gaps.

A couple of windows were boarded up. A lot of shingles on the roof were missing. Everything beyond the house was overgrown. From here, the smaller buildings were barely visible.

I loved this place with all my heart, chinks and all.

The house would look spectacular once it was fixed up. Never again would I worry about being thrown out. I was guaranteed a place to live for as long as I wanted. Tears welled in my eyes at the thought of never being at the mercy of a boyfriend who didn't care about me. No more packing in a flash or finding my stuff on the front lawn. Never again would I have to sleep in my car. It was the most amazing gift I could imagine.

The magic coursing through my veins hummed as if to welcome me home. I felt in my bones that I belonged here. Sure, the entire property needed some TLC, but it was mine. Thanks to Walter's extremely generous gift, I could make it over any way I liked.

Not the money. The *magic*.

Along with the will, keys, and financial records, Frank gave me Walter's spell book and extremely detailed instructions on how to keep it safe once I arrived. There was apparently a heavily spelled trunk upstairs, but I'd need this book to find it. Not just anyone could climb these stairs. I'd started poring over these pages before Frank even finished telling me what the book did.

One of many things this grimoire said was that my magic drew power from the earthy elements: home, thread, hearth. Which meant the remodeling spell on page three would do whatever I asked.

Theoretically.

Only one way to find out. Closing my eyes, I envisioned a dream castle I'd spotted online once. The majestic house had light-colored brick on the outside, which looked far less foreboding than this dirty dark gray. A stone staircase led up to the double doors, which sat below stained glass windows that must be twenty-five feet high.

I wrinkled my nose and recited the spell. Thunder crashed. A gust of wind knocked me backward. My butt hit the driveway, hard. Pretty sure I blacked out for a second.

When I opened my eyes, Pink stood in my lap, sniffing my nose. The roof now boasted a gaping hole in the middle.

"Did a meteor hit us?" I asked, realizing how it sounded.

"Your spell seems to have not worked as intended," Pink said mildly.

That was an understatement. My ribs throbbed like a horse had kicked them. If magic always felt this terrible, I was done. Finite. Audi five thousand.

Dazed, I looked around. "What happened?"

"Magic is fragile. Take your time and learn it in stages. You can't just wiggle your nose and have the universe shape itself to your liking."

"I see that now." I gestured to the house. "Can I fix this?"

"Luckily, yes. You should be able to undo the spell."

It took three tries with the book to get the words right, but eventually the house looked like when I got here. "Much better!"

Pink nodded. "Absolutely. Also, you look like Carrot Top stuck his finger in a socket."

"What?" With a groan, I checked my reflection in my car's side mirror. He wasn't entirely wrong. My normally wavy, newly red hair had puffed up into tight curls. My complexion appeared even paler than usual, and soot covered my cheeks. I definitely would not try that again. After swiping my face a few times, I left the smudges. This house had at least five showers. "Fine. Let's do this the slow way."

My not-helpful cat watched while I unpacked everything from my trunk and carried it up the porch steps. Once the rain started, I didn't want to trek across the driveway to get the rest of my stuff.

After I finished the last load, I slammed the trunk shut and motioned Pink to come inside with me. I didn't want my magic cat to get lost in the woods.

We were halfway to the front porch when a new-looking, shiny red BMW convertible turned into the driveway. In my surprise, I almost dove back into my Corolla before remembering I had every right to be here.

More than anyone else, in fact. Except maybe the cat.

The car stopped, and a woman exited. Her chin-length brown hair and pointed nose looked vaguely familiar, but I'd only met about four people since arriving in New York, and she wasn't one of them. Three, actually, since Pink wasn't a person. The lines on her face and gray streaks in her roots probably made her a few years older than me, putting her in her late forties or early fifties. She stood as if someone had tied a yardstick to her back.

"Can I help you?" I asked, hoping to sound official and not terrified.

"My name is Dottie Evans," she said, flashing a silver badge so quickly it might have been a Pop-Tarts wrapper. "I've been sent by the Office of Magical Enforcement to investigate excessive magical use in the area."

No way I'd heard her correctly. There couldn't be magical police. That wasn't a thing. Was it?

"The office of what?" I pasted a hopefully friendly smile onto my face. "I think I need to get my hearing checked."

"Most likely, you understood me just fine. It's not every

day a Magical Enforcement Office Witch pops up in your home," she said. "Don't you dare tell me what the acronym for that title is."

Pink meowed at her. I pressed my lips together to keep them from twitching.

"You've got that right. Forgive me. I didn't even know there was such a thing as Magical Law Enforcement. I suppose you don't go by your title, then? What should I call you?"

"Dottie is fine."

The name explained why she seemed so familiar. "Dottie Evans? Aren't you the local massage therapist? I passed one of your ads on the way here."

Her smile could only be described as condescending. "I can hardly walk around the town as a witch officer, can I? The OME primarily hires part-time enforcement. Only the top brass gets a full salary. They're really snooty about it, too. Call themselves the Witches' Council. I call them the Council of Witches. If my title spells MEOW, theirs can be COW."

I snorted. "Well, that seems fair."

"Anyway, I have bills to pay, and my magic lends itself to healing. I set up a practice by appointment only, which gives me the flexibility to close when duty requires. It also lets me get to know the townspeople. You'd be amazed what secrets people spill on the massage table."

"I bet I would," I said before realizing I was being rather inhospitable. "Can I offer you a cup of coffee? Or... water? I don't know if there's a coffeemaker in the stuff left for me. Or cups, now that I think about it. I haven't actually been inside yet. If you want to come back tomorrow, I'll be much more well-positioned to entertain."

"Thank you, no. Is there somewhere more private we could chat?"

With more than a little trepidation, I led her inside. How could I be in trouble with the witch police already? I'd only inherited my witch powers twenty-four hours ago. And, okay, I'd just attempted a significant renovation that left the house looking like a meteor struck, but I undid it. No one knew besides me and Pink.

Inside the doors, the view stopped me in my tracks. Whatever I'd expected, it wasn't a marble-tiled foyer with high ceilings and a curving staircase leading upstairs. Through double doors to the right, I saw what appeared to be a ballroom. An actual ballroom! I desperately wanted to check, but, well, witch police.

I stifled a gasp at the scene as Dottie narrowly avoided walking into me. "You haven't been in here before?"

"No, I just arrived."

"And you started doing magic immediately?" Her words filled me with shame. "Without even taking a peek inside? That's like salting your food before tasting it."

I directed my answer to the floor. "I guess I got excited. Look, I'm really sorry. I definitely learned my lesson with the massive lightning strike or whatever happened."

To my surprise, she smiled and led me to the sitting area. Although the place had been empty for decades, some of the antique furniture remained, waiting for me. Frank hinted that there may have been a spell or two preserving them. Considering that I owned exactly no furniture of my own, as long as I could sit, I didn't care.

Dust covers hid the furniture, but she whipped them off and dumped them on the coffee table in the blink of an eye. "Emma, please, sit."

I perched on the chair, mostly so she couldn't sit next to

me. She took the middle spot on the sofa. Dottie blocked my escape out of the room, but since she was a witch and my car was about thirty years older than hers, I didn't expect to make it far if I made a break for it.

Pink padded into the room before leaping onto the couch between me and Dottie. He sat on his haunches, watching.

"What's going on?" I asked.

"Well, first, the Office of Magical Enforcement likes to welcome new witches to the neighborhood."

"Thanks?" I didn't feel terribly welcome.

"I'm guessing you're new at this. Our records indicate this house used to belong to Walter Sparrow. Certain powers transferred to you when his will was settled."

I nodded, but said nothing.

"With magic comes responsibility. We're thrilled to have another witch join our ranks—you may not know this, but your grandfather was highly regarded in the community."

Thinking back to the Walter Sparrow Annual Memorial Treasure Hunt held in Shady Grove a few weeks ago, I said, "Yeah, I got that impression."

"Great! And you wouldn't want to destroy his legacy by alerting the entire state to a new witch in town within minutes of arriving in Willow Falls. Magic needs to be subtle. A little here, a touch there. You can't remodel an entire house in the middle of the day. Or, more accurately, cause a near-total collapse."

"Can I do magic at night when everyone is sleeping? This place is surrounded by trees. No one would know." Sure, the first spell backfired, but if at first you don't succeed...

She pressed her lips together and glared at me, but I

would've sworn she was trying not to laugh. "We'd prefer that you refrain from calling undue attention on yourself or on us. Your grandfather left you more than enough money to bring in licensed contractors. Also, you should know—magic is not good for structural changes. Not unless you are extremely powerful or have a particular talent in that area. Do you?"

"I'm not sure yet."

"Then I suggest you stick to the small stuff. Cosmetic updates, interior cleaning, and minor repairs. If another spell gone wrong destroys the property, we won't protect you. Is that understood?"

"Yes, ma'am."

Pink climbed onto her lap, curling into a ball. I braced myself for another lecture, but she smiled indulgently and scratched his ears. "And you. What's your excuse, Sir?"

Pink meowed up at her. With shock, I realized I couldn't understand him. Maybe he was playing cat...but then Dottie replied in French. My cat didn't want me to know what they were saying.

"Traitor," I muttered under my breath.

Dottie smiled, but didn't look at me again until they finished their conversation. She picked Pink up and set him gently on the floor, then turned back to me.

"Cat magic is a little different," she said. "Non-witches won't understand him unless there's a compelling need. You can speak with him most of the time, unless he's having a private discussion. Just a little protection against eavesdroppers. Don't blame Pink. He's a good cat."

He sat on the floor and lifted one leg, licking his rear paw as if to say, "Look at me! Just a normal feline!"

"Right. Good kitty," I said dryly.

"You two will get along fine," Dottie said while walking

toward the door. "But remember: magic is a privilege. Don't overuse it. And don't get caught by non-magic people. You don't want to face the consequences."

I stood in the doorway and watched her go, not sure what to say. After finding my new powers, of course I wanted to use them! That was totally normal.

What should I do now?

An unearthly scream answered my silent question.

Slowly, I turned, but nothing seemed amiss. "Pink? Did you hear that?"

"Oh, yes." He sounded amused. "Just wait."

Another yell, this one louder. Then I realized it wasn't a regular scream. Someone was yelling my name.

"Hello?" I called, still not moving from the door. "Is anyone there?"

An old man burst through the ballroom doors, headed straight for me.

I shrieked.

He came to a dead halt. "Emma! You're here!"

"How do you know me?" I asked. "Who are you? What are you doing here?"

"Isn't it obvious?" He bowed with a flourish, sweeping off an imaginary top hat as if dressed to the nines. In reality, he wore a tattered bathrobe, tied loosely over a white t-shirt and a pair of striped boxer shorts, plus a pair of brown house shoes that someone had sewn a bunny face onto. "This is so exciting! I've been alone forever."

My breath caught in my throat. I could see right through him.

TWO

A ghost. There was a ghost in my house. An old man ghost had come to kill me. I should've known this was all too good to be true. I hadn't exercised in months. (Okay, fine: years.) I might manage to wrestle an old man to the ground if he were alive, but how did a person tackle a ghost?

Wait. Run.

I could outrun a ghost. Maybe. How did ghosts move?

Before I could figure out what to do, the ghost continued talking to me like any of this was normal. "It's so nice to finally meet you."

I swallowed my instinct to race through the door, get in my car, and peel out as fast as possible in a car that went from zero to sixty in about four minutes. I could handle this. After all, I was a witch. Pink was a talking cat. Ghosts weren't that out there. Not like, say, aliens.

"Not to be rude, but who are you? What are you doing in my foyer? And also, I don't know a polite way to ask this but—are you dead?"

He tipped his head back and cackled. "Of course I'm

12

dead! You thought your dear old granddad was still alive after all this time? Hosting an annual treasure hunt to locate my heir during life would be my kind of eccentric, I suppose, but no. I used more conventional methods of trying to find you until my last day. Now here you are! It's wonderful! So nice to finally meet you."

It took longer than it should have for his words to sink in. Then I felt ridiculous for not realizing immediately who was the most likely person to be haunting this space. "You're my grandfather? Walter Sparrow?"

"In the flesh! Well, ghostly flesh, I suppose." He poked at himself, hand going right through. "I'd offer to shake hands, but, well, I'm not entirely sure how to accomplish that."

My mind was still having trouble with the whole scenario. "You've been living here all this time?"

"Of course I have. Where do you think I would go? I'm dead. Not a lot of hot spots welcoming ghosts these days."

I shrugged and gestured vaguely upwards. "Into the light? I don't know. To be honest, I hadn't given it a lot of thought."

"Oh, no. Far too much to do. Or, I thought there was. Turns out I can't really affect the world around me. Being a ghost is pretty boring most of the time."

"I'm sorry," I said. Then I remembered my manners. "Thank you for all of this. You have no idea how much I appreciate it. It's nice to finally meet you, Grandpa."

"Oh no, dear. Don't do that. Walter, please. Or Walt. My friends used to call me Brando after the late, great Marlon. There was quite a resemblance when we were both younger. Not toward the end, of course."

As odd as it would feel to address anyone as Marlon Brando, directing it at my grandfather seemed twice as awkward considering how many times I'd watched *A Streetcar Named Desire* in college. I'd stick with Walter, thanks.

"Gosh, it's nice not to be alone anymore. Oh, and you look just like your grandmother. Same red hair, same hazel eyes. You got my bone structure, though."

My hand went self-consciously to the loose bun I'd piled on top of my head so it wouldn't be in the way while moving boxes. Although I'd seen old pictures of my grandmother, most were in black-and-white.

"You really can't leave the house at all?"

"Sadly, no. I would give anything to travel around, talk to people like I used to. You're the first person who's seen me."

Oh, that made me sad. "Really? Not a single person in all this time? Do all magical people see ghosts? Or do you think it's because we're related?"

He shrugged. "There's no instruction manual. Right after I died, I tried to talk to my housekeeper, who was still here, and the lawyer. No one but Pink ever replied. But they weren't magic. I guess we'll find out. Invite some people over!"

"Sorry, I don't know too many people around here yet." I thought for a minute. "What happens when you try to leave?"

"I just find myself in the ballroom. It's a beautiful room, but your cat here refuses to play the piano for me."

"I'm a cat," Pink said.

"Where would you go first if you could leave?" I asked.

"Ooh, good question! I hear they're doing *Jersey Boys* in Albany. I'd love to see that again. Brilliant show."

"Do you know why you can't leave?"

He shook his head. "Wish I did."

"Did you choose to be a ghost, or did it just happen? Can anyone be a ghost?"

"I think I'm here to help you."

"How?"

"So I can impart my wisdom, of course. Help you grow into your own as a witch. Teach you about this world that you never knew about."

I gestured to my cat. "I thought that's what Pink was for."

Walter snorted. "Cats don't have a moral compass."

"Shows what you know," Pink said. "Just because I didn't want to lure people into the house for you to scare them—"

"Can you do that? Scare people?"

"No idea. Maybe? It would definitely be worth finding out. I'd like to meet other ghosts, too. Haven't seen even one in all this time. But that doesn't mean they aren't around," he said.

"A fair point. I wonder if I'd be able to see them."

"As far as I'm concerned, you are a one-ghost woman. I'm not in the mood to share my granddaughter. It's been a lonely few decades, but now that you're here, we'll have all sorts of fun! We can host sleepovers and parties and—oh! You know what I've always wanted to do? Run a murder mystery dinner! Let's do that! Quick, invite all your friends."

His excitement was both contagious and terrifying. As much as I was thrilled to meet my grandfather at long last —even if he was a ghost—I also wasn't exactly prepared to turn my new place into party central before I finished moving in. "One thing at a time. I haven't even unpacked yet."

"Hmmph. What are you waiting for? Come on, I'll show

you to your room!" Before I could respond, he floated toward the staircase. Then he vanished and reappeared at the top. "Boo!"

A laugh escaped me. Of all the things I expected when learning about my grandfather's legacy, an excited ghost with a playful side never occurred to me. Life was about to get a lot more interesting.

"You better follow him," Pink said. "He's literally got nothing to do but come down and talk to you until you go look at whatever he wants to show you."

Shaking my head, I headed up the stairs so a ghost and a talking cat could give me a tour of my new life. What a world this had become.

Two months later...

Excitement filled the air. Every surface in the mansion gleamed. The phone lines and Wi-Fi were installed, which shouldn't have been the most exciting part of starting a new business, yet somehow had been. My website went live yesterday, and today, we opened our doors. I'd even put a batch of cookies in the oven to fill the air with the delightful smell of baked goods as people entered.

"Please don't let today be completely dead," I said, half to myself and half to Pink. He'd jumped onto the shiny wooden counter I'd installed in the foyer to greet guests and settled down to watch the doors. Lucky for him, I'd gone with Dottie's advice and hired a professional rather than conjuring his perch out of thin air.

The words had barely left my mouth when the front

door flew open and my seventy-five-year-old neighbor stormed in. "You, girl! What do you think you're doing?"

Holding my ground, I met his gaze firmly. "Last month, I turned forty-two. I would appreciate it if you addressed me as Emma. I'm not a girl by any stretch."

"You are compared to me. And you didn't answer the question." He clutched something in his fist, waving it around in front of me.

"I'm opening my new bed-and-breakfast, Toby," I said calmly. "We talked about this."

"Have you ever heard the phrase, *be careful what you wish for*?" Pink asked.

"You hush," I whispered out the side of my mouth.

"What is this flyer?" Toby shoved it under my nose emphatically, as if he'd caught me doing something wrong.

Once I smoothed the paper out enough to recognize it, I knew exactly what it was. However, Toby's demeanor didn't give me much interest in mollifying him, so I scrutinized the page as if I hadn't hung it on the announcement board at the General Store last week.

"You took my sign down?"

"Well, no. I copied it and put it back up. But you're avoiding the question!"

"It's a job posting. Are you here to apply?" I asked sweetly.

He harrumphed at me. "You should be so lucky."

"If I recall correctly, your B&B doesn't serve lunch or dinner. I'm not competing against you for those meals. Maybe we could help each other, Toby. Be neighborly? Tell you what. I'll give you coupons for your guests to give ten percent off once we get the restaurant up and running. No, twenty."

"Please don't poke a sleeping bear," Pink said. "We

spent so much time trying to find someone to take over the legacy, and I'd hate to start over because the neighbor throttled you. Unless you have kids?"

Toby opened and closed his mouth, which made his thick, white eyebrows dance. It might have been funny if I wasn't worried he would give himself apoplexy in my foyer.

"Can I get you a glass of water?" I asked with as much sweetness as a person can inject into those words.

Finally, he jabbed a finger in my direction. "You're just lucky I knew your grandfather, girlie."

"You realize I'm not doing anything wrong, right? This home was licensed as a B&B before I inherited it. We filed all the paperwork to finish probate and transfer ownership. Contractors came over to fix things up and make it safe. The house is mine, and the intended use falls within applicable zoning regulations." Walter's lawyer must have expected Toby's objections to me taking over because he'd handled everything before I even knew there could be problems. Thank goodness for Frank.

"But did you get the building permits for the work?" Toby asked.

I paused and tilted my head. My eyes widened. "Permit? Gosh, what's a permit?"

"A-ha! I knew it!"

With a laugh, I pulled a handful of papers out from under the desk. "Come on, Toby. Give me some credit. I wasn't born yesterday."

"Don't mock me, girl." He stepped toward me, hands curling into fists.

Pink moved between us and arched his back, hissing. Toby looked down at him, but you didn't have to be a witch to understand that statement.

"If you're going to scare my cat, I'm going to have to ask you to leave," I said. "All of this is perfectly legal."

"Oh yeah? I guess we'll see about that, won't we?" He spun on his heel, rushing out as fast as he'd come in.

I checked the spot where he'd been for skid marks.

"That interesting enough for you?" Pink asked.

"Hush. He's just mad that he's not the only game in town anymore. He can't know that we aren't really competition for him."

When I inherited Walter's estate, I also received his legacy of helping others. To pay his gifts forward and make the world a better place, I'd established this property as a B&B. I wanted people to come and go with no one looking too closely. But for most people staying here, there was no fee. My goal was to help people find themselves, the same way I'd found my calling when my magic arrived. All I asked was that people helped around here in whatever capacity they could.

Toby might not be happy to hear that most of my rooms cost nothing, though. If he thought I was stealing his customers, knowing that it was impossible to undercut my rates might make matters worse.

After the door closed behind Toby, I took a deep breath and tried to reclaim my opening day excitement. I could do this. There was only one tiny wrinkle: my dismal food offerings. Even Walter found them repulsive, and he couldn't smell or taste anything.

The high ceilings and spacious, fabulously redesigned rooms might bring guests into my new B&B, but the noxious odors from my disastrous efforts at cooking would send them out faster than you could say, "Emma is the world's worst chef." If I really wanted to help people, the goal was to offer a place to stay and food that wouldn't poison them.

And I badly wanted to make this place successful. It had been a joy to come here and discover a real knack for hearth magic: making beds and cleaning and doing dishes were fun now! Even renovating was a breeze. But apparently cooking was a different type of magic, and old granddad hadn't left me that particular talent.

It's cool. I didn't mean to sound ungrateful.

Being able to use my magic for a lot of the cleaning and updating saved me time and allowed me to open much faster than a non-magic person could. It also gave me extra funds to stimulate the local economy. My plan had been to buy my guests baked goods from the local farmers market to satisfy the "breakfast" half of "bed-and-breakfast." Unfortunately, I'd been recently reminded that we lived in upstate New York now. The market closed for winter in a couple of months. Hence the ad that brought Toby in here in such a tizzy.

The smoke alarm interrupted my thoughts.

A curse escaped me as I ran into the kitchen. I'd completely forgotten about my bright idea of offering warm cookies at the entrance for guests, like a Doubletree. Their cookies didn't catch fire.

A gust of smoke caught me in the face when I opened the door. Coughing, I waved it away and shot a spell to open the window.

Pink watched me with an amused look while I pulled the now-ruined batch of cookies out of the oven and dropped them with a clatter in the sink. I know, I know, but he did. This lucky black cat did a lot of things regular cats couldn't. Too bad he couldn't bake.

I glanced at him. "Do you want to try? Your cookies can't come out worse than mine."

He lifted a paw and licked it with great leisure. "Why are you doing it the difficult way? Baking in the oven is so human."

"In case you hadn't noticed, I am human. We can't all be cats."

"You're not human. You're a witch."

An excellent point, but not necessarily a useful one. Hands on my hips, I examined the blackened lumps in my sink. To call them cookies would be an insult to the good people at Toll House. I hadn't tried any cooking spells yet, but I'd learned a lot. Since moving in, I'd really come into my witchy powers.

The thought made me grin. I loved having witchy powers.

If there was a specific spell to make ruined cookies edible, Walter's book didn't mention it. But maybe I could feel it out. With a pair of oven mitts, I gingerly pulled the tray out of the sink and scooped the cookies onto a plate. Then I closed my eyes, squished my nose twice like Samantha from *Bewitched*, and pictured a plate of gorgeous, mouth-watering creations. In my mind's eye, they smelled so good, I could almost taste them.

After about thirty seconds, Pink's amused voice cut into my concentration. "You might as well look. Standing there won't change anything."

Tentatively, I peeked out through my half-raised lids. Then I clapped and let out a squeal of delight. Cookies! Grabbing one, I took a huge bite. What beautifully golden, perfectly rounded cook—lumps of charcoal.

With a cough, I spit the horrific mess into the sink. Oh, that was beyond disgusting.

"Not what you were going for?" Pink asked.

"Well, they look good." I offered a hopeful smile. "That's half the battle, right?"

"I could've told you they smelled like something died."

"Next time, would you?"

Without waiting for him to respond, I went to the cupboard and pulled out the largest glass I owned. It took four gulps of milk before the charcoal taste left my mouth. When I finished, I returned to the foyer to check my email and make sure everything looked perfect while I waited to interview potential cooks.

Not a single guest came in before my phone alarm told me to expect the first interviewee in a few minutes. I took a moment to check my waves in the mirror behind the front desk. My whole life, I'd been strawberry blonde, but when Walter's magic arrived, it was like my hair went Technicolor. I loved it. Not a hair out of place, thanks to my new smoothing spell. Which reminded me. Looking down, I said a quiet spell to remove a wrinkle from my suit and—

Three knocks sounded firmly on the front door. Punctual. I liked that. She didn't have to knock on the door of a public business, but I wouldn't fault someone interviewing for a job for being polite.

Opening the door, I found a severe-looking woman who appeared to be about sixty standing on the front porch. Gray hair skinned back tightly into a bun, wire-rimmed glasses on the tip of her nose. She wore a dark pink chef's jacket, black pants, and kitchen shoes. No jewelry other than a small diamond ring on her left hand and matching gold wedding band. Simple.

When my gaze got to her feet, she clucked her tongue, and I realized she'd been giving me the same once-over. "Flip-flops in the kitchen? That will never do!"

Opening a job interview with an insult to the potential employer seemed an odd choice, but fortune favors the bold, right? Holding out one hand, I pasted a smile on my face. "I'm Emma. I don't cook; that's why I need you. You must be Martha."

"I don't know if I must be, but I am." She gestured to the interior, reminding me I was blocking her entrance. "May I come in, or will we conduct the interview out here?"

Blushing furiously, I apologized and led her into the kitchen.

She gave the air an exaggerated sniff. "If this is the best your other applicants can do, I arrived in the nick of time."

With a deep breath, I reminded myself that Martha was both highly qualified for this position and also one of only two applicants. Also, I was the boss here. Time to take charge of the interview. "Why don't we take a seat? I've been looking over your résumé—"

"Résumé, schésumé! What does that tell you about a person?"

"Ooh, she's a spitfire," Walter said. It took everything in me not to jump when he appeared at my elbow. I was getting better, but it was quite jarring. "You could use someone like her to keep you in line."

Since I couldn't respond, I scrutinized Martha's resume. It did not disclose her demeanor, that's for sure. "Well, in this case, it tells me you studied at the Culinary Institute of New York. That's an excellent school."

"It most certainly is. I've spent the last twenty years cooking for the military. When I retired last month, I moved to Willow Falls to be with my grandchildren."

"That sounds nice."

"Incredibly dull, the lot of them. I'm bored to tears. They all want me to 'rest' and 'relax' and some such nonsense. Last week, my daughter-in-law tried to take me to a spa!" She said that with the same horror I'd use if someone asked me to stroll through the sewers. "I need something to do with my days, and I'm not very grand-motherly."

Perhaps the first thing she'd said that I agreed with. "Well, I can help you with that. Right now, I'm looking for someone in the mornings. But if business goes well, I'd love to expand to lunch and dinner."

"Dinner? Isn't this a bed-and-breakfast?" She peered past me as if she could see through the kitchen door to the rest of the house.

"It is, but there's an enormous dining room. Plenty of room to set up tables, hire a full staff, and serve other meals. If we get there, you'll be able to help with hiring additional staff. But one thing at a time. I'd love to taste what you can do. Make me your best eggs."

"Eggs?" Walter made a gagging noise. "Oatmeal, that's what you need! It'll give you strong bones, like me. And lots of energy to help you live a long life."

While I felt sorry for my grandfather, alone in this house all this time, his commentary was making me dizzy.

"Let me make you my special protein-filled breakfast." Martha went to the large fridge and gestured toward the doors. "May I?"

When I nodded my consent, she pulled out a carton of eggs, a jug of milk, and a rasher of bacon. The bacon, at least, endeared her to me. Then she found the bread drawer and moved toward the stove.

As she worked, Martha told me about her extensive experience cooking for the military. She was unquestion-ably qualified. The pans on the oven sizzled and steamed, filling the air with delicious smells.

24

With a wave of my hand, I removed the lingering burnt-cookie odor. Hopefully, she'd think she'd gotten used to it or it went away on its own.

"Normally I would make my award-winning cinnamon rolls," she said. "Blue ribbon at the County Fair, seven years running. Unfortunately, they need to rise for several hours."

Fifteen minutes later, she set a gorgeous plate in front of me. Sizzling bacon, sitting next to some beautifully golden scrambled eggs. Toast that had been grilled to perfection sat on either side, cut into perfect diagonals. After the cookie incident, I hadn't been hungry, but now my mouth watered. Picking up my fork, I took a bite.

The eggs were delicious. Possibly the best eggs I'd ever tasted. They were buttery and fluffy. The bacon was the perfect amount of crunchy without being overcooked. The toast melted in my mouth. I wanted to sit here for the rest of my life and eat everything Martha made.

But I didn't like her. Could I get over that?

This was my first time running a business, and my first time hiring employees. None of my prior jobs granted me any sort of responsibility. Most of them only lasted a couple of weeks. A month ago, my life was a disaster. Every job I tried turned out miserably. I'd never even dreamed of finding my calling—I would have given my back teeth to do anything as well as Martha cooked. She would do an excellent job if hired, no question.

At the same time, my chef would be here five days a week. We'd spend a fair amount of time together. Did I want someone who judged me and insulted me? Could we become friendly over time? Or would she drive me up the wall until I wanted to strangle her?

CHAPTER

THREE

After oohing and ahhing over the food again, I thanked Martha for her time and let her know I'd be in touch soon. Even if she wasn't a good fit for the bed-and-breakfast, she was a talented cook, and I wished her well.

"You're not going to hire her, are you?" Walter appeared at my elbow, close enough that we'd be touching if he wasn't incorporeal. I hated when he did that, but he still thought it was a hoot. "We prefer a bit more personality around these parts. Tell her to go."

"I'll let you know when I make my decision," I said loudly, with a pointed look at my ghost.

He hmmed and moved over to the couch, which was his favorite spot now that I'd put up a TV for guests. He loved old *Scooby Doo* reruns. Although it was a kids' show, it felt oddly appropriate.

Okay, fine. I liked it, too.

Ignoring him, I opened the door to walk Martha to her car. Another woman stood on the porch, preparing to knock. She appeared to be older than me, with graying brown hair cut into a bob. In stark contrast to Martha, she hunched over as if not wanting to take up too much space.

Martha visibly recoiled at the sight of her. "You!"

"Hello, Martha," the woman said.

"Do you two know each other?" To the newcomer, I said, "Hi, I'm Emma."

"I'm sorry to say we do," Martha replied. "If this is the type of person you welcome in your establishment, then we might not be a good fit."

Having already decided not to hire her unless the second applicant provided something inedible, that didn't seem an enormous loss. But I didn't want to be rude. "I believe Josefina is here to also apply for the chef job. You are her, right?"

"I am. Please, call me Josie," she said.

"Hmmph." Martha swept past her and headed across the porch to her car without so much as another goodbye.

"It's nice to meet you," I said, offering to shake hands.

She took it limply, barely touching me before pulling back. It was all I could do not to check to see if my hands were dirty. A dark spot peeked out from beneath her jacket. When she saw me looking, she pulled it down. "You, too. Sorry about that. It's a small town. Everyone knows each other. We're not exactly friends."

Part of me wanted to reassure her that Martha and I weren't friends either, but that would be as unprofessional as asking her to spill the tea on their relationship. Which I also wanted to do. Instead, I said, "Let me show you to the kitchen."

She walked a few steps behind me, eyes taking everything in. Her entire demeanor put my spidey senses on high alert. Josie acted like a scared rabbit about to go skittering down the road. All of a sudden, I didn't care if she could cook or not. I wanted to take her in, ask her to stay, wrap her in a weighted blanket, and offer hot cocoa. So what if it was August?

Hoping to put her at ease, I went to the island and offered her a stool. "Tell me about your cooking experience. Where did you train?"

"I'm self-taught," she said. "I know how that sounds, but I love food."

To be honest, her response didn't inspire a lot of confidence in me. It was less what she said than how she said it. This woman suffered from a huge lack of confidence.

Some people weren't great at selling themselves. Her sample dish might still melt in my mouth. Hopefully.

When she dropped the first knife, that made me nervous. Thankfully, she avoided her toes. When the second knife fell, I whispered a quick spell to help it clatter safely to the tile floor instead of landing on her right foot.

"Is everything okay?" I asked.

"Fine. I'm just nervous. I'm sorry."

"It's okay. Listen, if it helps, pretend I'm not here." I hated to say it, but I didn't quite trust that she wouldn't set the place on fire if left to her own devices. It was already clear who the better applicant was, despite my personal feelings toward each of them.

To her credit, once she got into the groove, Josie managed to create a plate of eggs that were egg-colored. They were runny and somehow overcooked at the same time. Although I liked my bacon on the rare side, if I snapped my fingers, I was pretty sure I could turn this batch back into a pig.

The choice was obvious. I didn't have a lot of time to keep looking, and there was really no need: I had one highly qualified candidate already.

When she set the plate in front of me, Josie apologized, not meeting my eyes. I reached out and touched her arm, and she flinched. "I should go."

"No. Why don't you sit for a minute, and we'll chat?" I said. "I'll make coffee."

"No, no, it's okay. This was a bad idea. I'm horribly embarrassed. I should have known better. My food never comes out right when I'm stressed. Seeing Martha threw me. But I saw this job came with a room and I needed a place to stay and I'll get out of your hair now. Sorry for wasting your time."

"Wait!" I didn't know what this woman's story was, but she clearly needed someone to help her. "I don't want you to go. I want to give you a job."

She smiled sadly. "As much as I appreciate the gesture, if you tell me those are good eggs, I'm going to have to call your mother and chat about telling lies. Something went terribly wrong with that dish, and we both know it."

I snorted as I pushed the plate away. "No, I respect you too much to pretend. Also, I don't want to eat them just to be nice. But there are many jobs here and plenty of space. Can you answer phones? Run a check-in counter? Make beds or sweep?"

It would take me roughly three seconds per room to put everything back together after each guest checked out, but Josie didn't need to know that. Until she felt comfortable with me, I ran a safe, normal bed-and-breakfast where no one used any magic.

"I don't want to take advantage of you," she said.

"It's not taking advantage when I'm offering you a job. You said you need a place to stay. Get your things and move in. The rest is details. We'll work that out after lunch. I mean, after I order lunch." I didn't want her to think she should cook another meal for me.

"Are you sure?"

"Yes, one hundred percent," I said.

"My bags are in the car." She spoke in a rush, like I might change my mind if she took a second to breathe between words. "I'll be right back!"

And just like that, instead of one employee, I had two. Or I would, as soon as I spoke with Martha. Two employees, one cat, and a Walter. Maybe Willow Falls wouldn't be as lonely as my old life.

When I turned to leave the kitchen, a pair of green eyes glowed at me out of the kitchen cupboard. I jumped about three feet. "Pink! How did you get in there?"

I reached for my naughty cat, but he swatted at me.

"If you're going to be like that, I'll put child locks on the cupboards," I warned.

"Maybe you should if you're just going to let anyone off the street wander in."

"It's a bed-and-breakfast. Taking in people off the street is literally what we do. Walter wants me to help people, remember?"

He lifted one paw in his way that always suggested he was giving me the finger. "Irrelevant. There's something off about that woman. And she can't cook! How can you hire a breakfast chef who makes liquid-yet-burnt eggs? If that's what you want, save money and do it yourself."

I couldn't even get offended at his review of my abilities. "She's not going to make breakfast. I'll call Martha and offer her the job. But Josie needs us. I can feel it. Remember Aly?"

"Annoyingly perky psychic who thought she could take your house? Yes, of course."

"She's only annoyingly perky if you're a cranky old cat," I retorted. "Anyway, she thought my powers had to do with helping people resolve unfinished business. Josie's clearly got some. Lank hair, bags under her eyes. Extremely skittish. There's a story there. Maybe she can't cook, but this is a big house. I'll find something for her to do."

Pink stared at me for so long it made me twitchy. Weren't cats supposed to be terrible at staring contests? I couldn't stand to be the one to end our eye contact, but finally I broke the silence. "What? Is there something on my face?"

"It's admirable that you want to help people. Walter is going to be proud."

"Thank you." His words filled me with such an unfamiliar feeling, it took me a minute to recognize the pleasure I took in making my family happy.

"With that said, Walter could be overly trusting, even naïve. I just want to make sure you keep your eyes open."

In the foyer, Josie called my name. I called back to reassure her before turning to my cat. "I'll be careful."

"See that you are. If you leave Walter alone for another twenty-six years, I'll never hear the end of it."

I blew him a raspberry on my way out the door. As if a cat would live another twenty-five years. Although, now that I thought about it, he was already at least thirty. Much, much older than your average cat, without a gray hair in sight.

After leaving Pink, I took Josie to the winding staircase that separated the entry from the dining area. It was my favorite feature of the house.

"Do you have any first-floor rooms?" Josie asked as I put my foot on the first step.

"I do, but I figured those would be for the guests. That

way, you don't have to worry about someone peeking in at you from the porch."

"I prefer not to have to climb the stairs," she said. "If it's all the same to you."

"Of course. Right this way. At the moment, I'm the only one living here, so there are plenty of options. I'll be hiring a cook, as you know."

"Oh, no. I can't ask you to give me someone else's room. If it's spoken for—"

"You're not asking. My grandfather gave me this enormous house, and I rattle around in it most of the time. There are plenty of rooms for you and Martha both." Having other people around would curb my constant redecorating, but I could live with that. "Besides, I get tired of talking to myself all day. You'd be doing me a favor, really."

"If you're sure," she said. "But I'm not taking any charity! Put me to work. I'll wash dishes. I'll clean, I'll make myself useful. Promise."

"And you'll accept a fair salary," I said. I could afford to treat my staff well. "Plus the room. Come on, I'll show you to your room."

We passed by the formal ballroom to get to the bedroom suite. I still had to pinch myself every time I saw the high ceilings, the fancy tile, the piano in the far corner. Leaving that door shut, we went down the hall to a set of closed double doors. According to the lawyer, these rooms belonged to my grandfather at the end of his life—it was a full suite. Bedroom, attached bath, sitting area. Since arriving here, I'd only gone in a couple of times. It wasn't remotely ready for guests.

In the hands of a regular person, that would be a problem. Hand on the door, I silently uttered a spell used several times over the past few weeks. As I turned the knob with one hand, I coughed and discretely snapped my fingers before pushing the door open.

Instantly, the room transformed. Instead of a stripped bed and drop cloths protecting the furniture, the room now contained a king-sized four-poster bed with two matching wooden nightstands. A massive mahogany dresser gleamed under a giant mirror without a speck on it. On the other side of the room sat a full living area, with a full-sized blue couch with cream and blue throw pillows beside a matching armchair. The open floor-length navy drapes revealed enormous windows and French doors leading to the patio.

Behind me, Josie let out a squeal of delight. "This is my room? You're joking, aren't you? This must be your suite."

Her obvious joy made me smile. "No, my room is on the top floor. I took the entire attic for myself. It's got an attached bath, a sitting room, and a balcony with a gorgeous view of the grounds, just like this. I like being up high."

"You've got good knees," she said. "Just wait. In ten years when you change your mind, I'm not giving this up."

"Deal," I said. "How soon do you want to move in? As you can see, your room is ready now."

"Oh, I can settle in today. I don't have a lot of stuff. There was a fire at my place, and I only saved a few things. I haven't even replaced most of my clothes yet."

My eyes moved up and down over her. "Lucky for you, I'm a bit of a seamstress. I've got some things that should fit you. Why don't you rest, and I'll go get them?"

She looked like someone had told her it was Christmas and *Star Wars* Day rolled into one. My heart went out to this woman—no home, clearly running from something. She obviously didn't want to talk about it, and that was okay.

When Aly told me that my gift was to help people resolve unfinished business, I hadn't quite believed her. Now, helping Josie seemed the most natural thing in the world. Even more natural than snapping a few sets of clothing into existence and acting like I'd run up and down the stairs to get them.

Becoming a witch was the best thing that had ever happened to me.

CHAPTER

FOUR

After leaving Josie to get settled, I called Martha to offer her the job. Explaining that someone she hated would also be living on the premises required some finesse, but my gut told me that Josie needed me to cut her a break. If that meant my cook and my desk person avoided each other, so be it.

Martha accepted the position immediately. "Of course you made the right choice. I knew you would. Now listen, my understanding is you provide room and board, is that right?"

"That's right."

"I don't need them. I prefer to continue living with my family. However, I will require additional pay to offset the expense."

"Not a problem." I reminded her of the salary range, and it only took a minute to reach an agreement.

"Excellent. I will start tomorrow. See you at four-thirty."

"I was hoping you'd be in early enough to prepare breakfast."

ADA BELL

She heaved a sigh. "Four-thirty *in the morning.*"

Good thing she couldn't see my flaming cheeks through the phone. "Right. I knew that. See you tomorrow."

She hung up before I could tell her about the mansion's newest resident. Ah, well. It would be better to break the news in person once she arrived.

Tinkling bells drew my attention away from my tablet to the front door. A very tall man with curly black hair stepped into the lobby. He wore jeans slung low over his hips, a soft-looking faded green t-shirt, work boots, and a hard hat. The color of the shirt made his brown eyes stand out. When he focused his gaze on me, something fluttered in my belly. Something I hadn't felt in quite a while.

"Welcome!" I said, noting his lack of luggage. "Are you looking for a room for the night?"

He shook his head and extended one hand. "My name is Cliff. I'm a contractor. I wanted to drop by, give you my card, see if you need any help with anything."

I did *not* need help remodeling, thank you very much. I could do all the remaining spells myself and—oh, wait. My hands were halfway to my hips when Dottie's warning rang in my ear. *No unnecessary magic!*

Who was the Office of Magical Enforcement to tell me what magic was necessary, anyway? A woman needed throw pillows! Probably shouldn't have tried to transform those cookies earlier, though, now that I thought about it.

Or cleaned up Walter's old bedroom. Or altered Josie's clothes. Oops.

Once I'd started, not using magic was hard.

Cliff was still looking at me, so I forced myself to pull it together. I struggled to come up with an answer that would both convey, "I am a strong, intelligent woman who doesn't

36

need a man for anything" and "please call me anytime, you good-looking stud."

Somehow, I settled on, "Do you live around here?" *Close enough to take me for drinks?*

Involuntarily, my eyes went to the ring finger of his left hand. Empty.

When did I start doing that? Twenty-year-old Emma rarely thought to ask if a guy she was interested in was married. I'd just assumed if they were flirting back, they must be available. Then again, that went badly more than once. Better to know upfront.

"Yeah." He gestured. "I'm right next door."

My hopes fell when I realized what direction he was pointing. "You're Toby's son."

"Guilty as charged."

"Does your father know you're consorting with the enemy?"

He chuckled. "Dad's all bark and no bite. He'd mad about having competition, but between you and me, I'm glad someone is finally pushing him into the twenty-first century. I've been nagging him for years to put up a website, allow people to book reservations online. Last week, he finally did it."

"I want the record to show that you didn't answer my question."

"You noticed that, huh?" His cheeks flushed. "Actually, Dad's exact words were something like, 'You're good with a hammer. Go see if the pretty girl next door needs anything done to her place.'"

That made me smile. "It's nice to know he doesn't totally hate me. Unless you're not a very good handyman."

"Twenty years' experience. Licensed and insured, with fair rates. Look me up online, you'll see. I do most of the work over at Dad's place, plus a few other homes in the area. I've always been good with my hands."

The words made my gaze go temporarily to the appendages in question, wondering exactly what skills they possessed. I forced the thought away. With a new business to run, dating wasn't a possibility right now. Especially not dating the son of a man who wanted nothing more than for me to board up my new B&B and leave town with my tail between my legs.

That thought reminded me of what Toby said about getting the appropriate building permits. Did he send his son to spy?

Whatever. Let him dig around. Toby would see there wasn't anything to find here.

"I've got a few projects that could use a professional touch."

"Great, thanks!" He handed me his card. "How is the kitchen? You got a commercial oven, sink, all the things you need to serve your guests?"

"It's not a full commercial kitchen yet, but I'm not quite ready to upgrade." He was looking at me so intently, I decided to take a chance. "I'd love to give you a tour, if you have a few minutes?"

"Oh, I don't want to be a bother."

"It's no bother. I'm just waiting for walk-ins. If anyone shows up, they can ring the bell." I pulled out a "Back in 10 minutes" sign from under the desk and set it on top of the counter beside a large, loud bell.

"Okay, then. Shall we?" He gave an exaggerated bow and held out one hand. It should have been corny, but he was cute enough that it worked. Or maybe it had just been too long since someone had paid attention to me like this.

Thankfully, Walter was nowhere to be seen. Showing

the handyman around was the closest I'd had to a date in over a year; the last thing I needed was my dead grandfather tagging along.

We started in the ballroom, which was by far the most impressive room of the house. With its high ceilings, marbled floors, and floor-to-ceiling windows, nothing else even came close.

Cliff gestured toward the full-sized grand piano near the far wall. "Do you play?"

"Oh, no. Not a note, unfortunately. It was here when I moved in."

"Did you buy the house recently? This place has been empty since I was a teenager. Dad didn't say anything other than that you might need some help."

"I inherited it from my grandfather when he died."

"Walter was your grandfather? I thought he never had kids."

"Surprise!" I smiled at him shyly. "It's a long story."

"Considering this place has been empty most of my life, I bet it is. What took so long?"

"There were some estate issues that needed to get settled," I said vaguely. Before he could push for more, I said, "I love this room."

Cliff said, "It's been kept up nicely. If I didn't know, I never would have guessed it fell into disuse."

The compliment made me beam, although I couldn't tell him why the ballroom looked the way it did back at the height of its use. Instead, I said, "Well, I want to be prepared when I'm ready for a party."

"Any idea when that would be?"

"You're not angling for an invitation, are you?" I grinned at him, hoping I wasn't misreading his intent.

"Maybe. Guess you'll have to send one and see if I

show." A beat later, he was back to business. "What's through that door?"

"A hallway to the back of the house. Those rooms aren't open to the public. It's a private living space. Other than needing some airing out, that part of the property is in pretty good shape. I'm not planning to do any work over there yet. Come on, let me show you the dining room."

We walked through the ground floor. Cliff examined everything, then stopped and shook his head when we got back to the foyer. "Forgive me for asking, but is there a bathroom down here?"

"Oh, sure." I pointed to a closed door. "It's shut now because it's not ready for guests. You can go right in through there. Sorry it's so small."

He chuckled. "No, I'm fine. I meant, if you're going to have a dining room for the public and a ballroom, your guests will need a place to relieve themselves that you don't feel the need to apologize for."

If we'd been chatting online, I would have sent him a face palm emoji. I'd been using my bathroom upstairs most of the time. Josie had her own, and most of the guest rooms shared. But obviously if I wanted this place to thrive as a public space, we would need decent facilities with running water on the ground floor.

"I guess it's a good thing you dropped by," I said. "Maybe you could give me an estimate?"

"Absolutely. Let me take some measurements. You'll need the door wide enough to fit a wheelchair, at a minimum. Plus some other modifications. I'll make a list for you. When should we get started?"

I shrugged. "Theoretically, I should have a public restroom down here as soon as possible. Even though people can use the ones upstairs, it doesn't make sense to delay. Besides, I wouldn't want non-guests roaming the halls. When are you free?"

"I'll swing by the hardware store, text you some pictures of what they've got. If the estimate works for you, we'll talk fixtures. As long as everything is in stock, we can start at the end of this week. I'm going camping with my buddy for a couple of days. I'll text you when I get back, and we'll go from there."

"Sounds good."

"Come on, girlie. Is that the best you can do?" Walter's gruff voice should have made me jump, but I held my expression intact when he materialized behind Cliff. Where did he come from? How did he do that? "Tell the man you're so sad I died, boo hoo, let him comfort you. He looks like someone great at comforting, if you know what I mean."

I knew but couldn't say so at the moment. Anyway, it was too late. Cliff was on his way out the door. It would be weird to call him back.

He left with a glance backward over his shoulder that made butterflies flutter in my stomach yet again. This was ridiculous. I reminded myself that I needed to add a bathroom, and talking about plumbing wasn't exactly flirting. Generally, I found restroom talk to be the exact opposite of romantic.

And yet. Some small part of my mind wanted to believe that maybe I wasn't just creating a home. Maybe I could have friends, a partner, and even a life here in Willow Falls. For the first time in a long time.

"Yeah, Walter. I know. And maybe one day, I'll find out."

FIVE

"Absolutely not!"

The screech of outrage shouldn't have reached my ears all the way up on the third floor, but I'd fallen asleep with my windows open and someone downstairs was furious. "I don't know who you think you are—"

That sounded like Martha. Rolling over, I grabbed my phone. It was seven-thirty in the morning. After letting my new chef in before dawn to start her breakfast pastries, I'd stumbled back up to bed to catch another hour or so of sleep. Apparently, I'd overshot a bit.

She should have been fine, a cook left alone in a commercial kitchen to make whatever she wanted. However, the crashes and yells coming from below me suggested otherwise.

A second person responded to the yelled words, too low for me to hear. I guessed Martha wasn't excited to meet her new co-worker.

Metal clanged. Another shriek. A cupboard slammed. At

this rate, they were going to wake up the entire neighborhood.

Another scream of outrage. The voices lowered a bit, and I started to relax. Maybe they would work things out on their own.

Then another voice joined the first. "Get away from me, or I'll kill you!"

Josie. Martha.

Enough was enough. Throwing back the covers, I raced for the door. There was no time to grab a robe, so good thing the pajamas I'd bought after moving in covered all the important bits. A month ago, I'd have been racing through the B&B in bikini panties and an old *Something Rotten* t-shirt.

I was halfway to the ground floor when Martha stormed out of the kitchen, past the bottom of the stairs. It took me a minute to recognize her because of the flour coating her entire body from head-to-toe. Rushing down the remaining steps, I called out to stop her.

"What's wrong? What happened?"

"That woman is trying to usurp my space! I cannot work under these conditions," Martha declared.

The only other person in the house was Josie. I couldn't imagine someone as meek as her trying to push Martha out of the kitchen, but I barely knew her. Even her shouted threat a moment ago sounded terrified.

"Let's calm down. We can work this out. Can I make you a cup of coffee?" I asked.

We'd almost made it to the marble floor at the bottom of the staircase when the kitchen door flew open a second time. Now Josie appeared in the doorway. Martha pointed and screeched. "She threw a bag of flour at me!"

That explained her appearance, yet nothing else. It

would take me less than a second to clean her up and restore her hair to the perfect bun she'd started with, yet somehow I didn't think bringing out my witchy powers was the way to resolve this dispute. Too bad I didn't have memory magic. I should ask Pink if that was a thing.

"Are you even listening to me?" Martha demanded.

"Yes, absolutely. I'm sorry. I just woke up. Let's sit down and talk. What happened?"

"There's nothing to talk about. I will not stay here while that woman is on the premises. My blueberry scones are in the oven. When the timer goes off, you pull them out. Do not overbake them." The look in her eyes made me fear that if I burned her scones, I might find myself an ingredient in the next batch.

"Got it."

"I'll return when she is gone," Martha announced.

"Wait! You can't leave! I need you to make breakfast." For me, at least. Mostly, I didn't want her to walk out and never come back.

"My scones will be delicious. Surely even you can make coffee."

Squeezing my eyes shut, I prayed for the ability to turn people into toads. When I opened my eyes, Martha still stood there, so again I tried to pacify her. "I understand that you're upset. Go home, take a breather. Come back this afternoon, and we'll talk about it. Once everyone calms down, the three of us can have a friendly conversation."

"Three? Oh, no! I will only return if she is gone." Whirling around, Martha stabbed her finger toward Josie, who was doing a great impression of the wallpaper.

"What happened?" I asked again.

Ignoring my question, Martha whipped off her apron

and threw it on the ground. Then she whirled around and went out the front door without another glance.

"What time will you be back?" I called as the door banged against the frame.

Nothing except the punctuating crash of the screen door.

This would never work. With a quick "Be right back!" over my shoulder to Josie, I ran after my cook. She was almost at her car when I caught up, panting. "Martha! Please wait! Tell me what happened, and I'll fix it."

"That woman was nosing around the kitchen, trying to find out what I put in my award-winning cinnamon rolls."

This was all about a recipe? Oh, dear.

"She was probably hungry," I said. "I told her you would start today, but she might not have realized that you were cooking for everyone, not just paying guests. Who we don't have yet."

"I'm not cooking for her!"

Something about her tone made me pause. "So I'm guessing you're not friends?"

Martha snorted. "As if I would be friends with a spy."

"What are you talking about? Josie's no more a spy than I am a toaster."

"From the day I won the blue ribbon at the County Fair, people have been trying to find out what's in my recipe. It is top secret. Not even my family knows. But recently, people have been asking to buy it. Nosing around. And now I see this woman boldly walk into my kitchen like she owns the place and start prying. I won't have it!"

Okay, things were coming together. This had all been based on a huge misunderstanding. Josie might have some secrets, but I didn't believe for a second she was some kind of cinnamon roll spy.

"Let me see if I understand," I said. "You were making your prize-winning cinnamon rolls—which sound amazing, by the way—when Josie entered the kitchen. She asked questions, and you didn't like the way she was peeking at your ingredients. Am I on the right track?"

"That's a lot of it, yes."

"I truly don't think she meant anything by it," I said, thinking fast. "Do you always need privacy when cooking or just when making your rolls?"

"Just the rolls." She sniffed and raised her head. "Although, to be honest, I'm not much into small talk. I prefer a quiet kitchen. But I refuse to work while that witch is in there, peeking over my shoulder."

For now, I ignored the insult to Josie. If I didn't handle this just right, I'd have to start the interview process all over. "That can be arranged. I have two options for you."

"I'm listening."

"Option 1: you give me a schedule. I tell everyone what time the kitchen is off-limits, then I make you a sign for each door. If anyone enters during those times, including me, you can throw us out. Option 2: you mix the dough at home, log your hours, and bring them here for baking. I will pay you for the time spent, even if you're not on site."

Martha thought for a minute. "I'm still a bit shaken. For today, I'd like to go home, make the dough, and come back. It's not far. You'll pay for travel time, too?"

"Sure." Anything to get her back here before guests started checking in and expected me to feed them.

"Usually I like to prep the dough in the morning, around eight-thirty. That way, they can rise when I'm done and go into the oven before lunch. If you can make me a sign for tomorrow, we'll see how things go."

"Thank you," I said desperately. "I very much appreciate it."

As she drove away, Pink appeared and rubbed up against my ankles. Crouching down, I scratched between his ears. "Don't you dare say 'I told you so.'"

"I wouldn't dream of it," he replied. "By the way, your scones are burning."

CHAPTER
SIX

Although I wanted to check on Josie, I needed to avoid burning the mansion down first. I opened the oven door, fanning the smoke furiously with one hand. With the other, I grabbed a potholder and yanked the burning scones out, tossing them into the sink.

It was getting thick in here. Coughing, I stumbled over to the kitchen door and pushed it open. Then I sent a teeny, tiny protection spell at my fire alarm so it wouldn't go off. Toby would be ecstatic to hear that the fire department got called to my B&B on our second day in business.

Once the air was relatively clear, and Pink had stopped gloating, I went to find Josie. She was in her room, stomping around furiously. A suitcase lay open on the bed, and she spoke rapid Spanish to no one I saw. When she spotted me, she stopped. Her face was pale.

"What just happened?"

She avoided eye contact. "I'm so sorry. I'll be out of your hair in half an hour."

"I don't want you out of my hair. I want to know what

set her off. She said you were trying to steal her recipe. What would make her think that?"

Josie laughed. "Oh, that's rich. As if anyone cares what she puts in those cinnamon rolls. You know, my friend Betsy used to say it must be drugs. Nothing else would make them so irresistible."

I snorted. "Well, it worked for the people at Coca-Cola. But, seriously, what happened?"

"I went into the kitchen to get breakfast. I forgot she would be here, honestly. Just wanted to find some cereal or toast. When I walked in, there were a bunch of bowls out on the counter. I went to see what you were making. Then Martha came out of the pantry, scaring the daylights out of me. She had an armload of ingredients. She started yelling at me to back off. Dumped everything on the counter and started waving her arms, insisting that Lydia wasn't going to get her recipe. Incidentally, that's how she got covered in flour. The bag poofed open."

"Who is Lydia?"

"I have no idea," she said. "Someone who likes cinnamon rolls, I guess? Don't tell Martha, but they're too sweet for me."

Trying to suppress a smile, I shook my head. This was clearly some huge misunderstanding, but it couldn't happen again. "I heard the two of you shouting all the way up in my room. I can't have that. You're lucky that there are only three of us this morning. There's no way I could have explained that commotion to guests."

"I understand." She bowed her head.

"The two of you are going to have to figure out how to get along. You don't need to become friends, but you have to be able to coexist peacefully."

"You're not firing me?"

"Why would I fire you? You didn't attack Martha, did you?"

She shook her head. "No, nothing like that."

"You're here because you needed a place to stay. I have empty rooms. The rest is details, and we can figure it out together," I said. "For now, I have a few things to do. When Martha comes back, I have to ask you to either try to get along or avoid her. I will ask her to do the same."

"I can do that. Thanks."

What a way to be woken up. With a groan, I realized I was still wearing my pajamas. I hadn't even taken the time to pull a robe on. After so many years of being on my own, I forgot that most people covered up in their homes around strangers. I'd have to remember that, especially if we were going to have anyone other than women over forty as guests.

Shaking my head, I headed up the stairs to my room. Martha wouldn't be back for a few hours, so I might as well go out and get a real breakfast for me and Josie. Something better than overcooked scones. Although we were technically open for business, I wasn't expecting anyone to come in.

A quick shower made me feel much better. After an internal debate about the weather, I pulled on my running shoes and headed for the trails behind the house. It was a warm morning and thunderclouds threatened in the distance, but my weather app swore it wouldn't rain until after lunch. That should give me plenty of time to get to the farmers market and back. Just to be sure, I grabbed an umbrella from the stand by the front door and tossed it into one of my reusable shopping bags.

The farmers market wasn't a terribly large operation—a handful of stalls with some picnic tables set up in the middle for people to sit and eat. But they sold the best strawberry rhubarb pie I'd ever had. (Full disclosure: before moving here, I hadn't been one hundred percent sure what rhubarb was. But I was an enthusiastic convert.) They also sold delicious muffins. Another stall offered a hot breakfast, but I didn't want to stay long enough to eat, and it would be cold before I made it back to the mansion.

I spent a few minutes gazing at the mouth-watering display of blueberry muffins, cookies, pie, and fresh jam before my stomach growled. The sound made me jump.

"Did you forget to eat breakfast?" the owner asked with a smile. We'd met a few times. The thirty-something woman ran this stall with her sister, although they looked so opposite I hardly believed they were related. Where this woman had long black hair, dancing eyes, and an easy smile, her sister wore her blond hair closely cropped and didn't speak unless directly addressed. The produce was grown on their family farm, about three miles down the road. In the fall, they opened up their pumpkin patch to guests.

I sighed. "Yeah. I'm starving. Everything looks so good!"

"I don't think we've been properly introduced. I'm Beth. You live around here?"

"Emma," I said. "I turned my grandfather's old house into a bed-and-breakfast not far from here. I just hired a cook, but she got into it with one of my other employees, and I didn't wind up getting to eat this morning."

"Martha works for you?"

That surprised me. "You know her?"

She shrugged. "I know everyone around here. Martha stopped by right when we opened. Didn't say where she worked, just that she'd taken a job in the area and needed a few things for breakfast. Got a big bunch of blueberries. The only places nearby are yours and Toby's, but Toby does his own baking. Martha and my sister got into an argument. I didn't hear what it was about, but after they started shouting, I had to get in the middle. Both of them stormed off."

The back of the stand where Beth's sister normally sorted and packaged goods for sale stood empty. This was the first time I'd been here without seeing both of them at work. It felt unnatural.

"I'm sorry about that. Is she around?"

Beth glanced back. "She must have gotten distracted. I thought she'd be back a while ago. Anyway, Lydia will be fine."

Lydia. I knew that name. Martha mentioned her when accusing Josie of spying.

I wrinkled my brow. "She doesn't make cinnamon rolls, does she?"

"I wish," Beth said. "Lydia can't compete with Martha's recipe, so she never makes them. The whole thing is ridiculous, if you ask me. There's room in this world for many types of goodies."

"Amen to that. When you see your sister, please apologize for me," I said. "Martha is a brilliant cook, but she needs time to adjust to sharing a kitchen. I'll talk to her."

"Be gentle. She might bite your head off, too. Over the past few weeks, I've gotten kind of used to seeing it on top of your neck where it belongs."

"To be honest, I'm partial to it myself. Only head I've got."

A clock beside the register caught my eye. I'd been gone too long. Quickly, I gathered up a selection of baked goods that would feed us for two or three days, even if Martha didn't come back. Then I paused. More people might show up. I couldn't turn anyone away because I didn't have breakfast, and I'd rather not come back. After a brief internal debate, I piled more baked goods onto the counter. Worst-case scenario, I'd snack on muffins all week.

The walk home took longer than necessary, partially because I enjoyed walking through the woods. This wasn't something I did a lot growing up in a suburb. Also, the longer I stayed out here, the more likely Josie and Martha might have resolved their differences by the time I got back.

When the mansion came into view, the first thing I noticed was my trusty old Toyota in the driveway. Toby was right it really was an eyesore. I could afford any car on the market, but it wasn't in my nature to throw something away just because it didn't look pretty. I supposed I could consider parking it in the barn around the side instead of right out in front. The driveway wasn't paved, but I could fix that.

A second car sat beside mine. At first I thought it was Josie's, but she'd parked on the far side of the building, closer to her room. When I recognized the vehicle as the one Martha had left in earlier, a huge smile crossed my face. She'd come back!

Please, please, please let her be coming to bake and not ask for her five hours pay before leaving forever, I silently begged.

It would be worth not needing any of the pre-made food I'd just picked up if my cook had returned to stay.

Instead of hauling all this stuff through the foyer, I followed the porch around to the kitchen door. Since my hands were full, I knocked, hoping Martha would let me in. No one answered. It took some juggling, but eventually I managed to balance my goodies on one knee long enough to pull the door open a few inches. I jammed a foot inside the gap, calling again for someone to help me.

Music blasted through the opening. It sounded like the kind of operas my grandmother used to listen to, although I wasn't familiar enough with the genre to tell anything else. Martha must have brought a radio with her or found one in the pantry. Good—if listening to music while she worked put Martha in a good mood, I was all for it.

Walter appeared, which I appreciated although he couldn't open the door. "You better hurry."

"Thanks," I said dryly. "Because I was trying to move as slowly as possible carrying all this stuff."

"I mean it," he said. "Get in there."

His tone made me nervous. Since I would get in much faster with some assistance from a human, I called inside the door again.

Still no answer. Maybe Martha was off making up with Josie. Or maybe she couldn't hear me over the Italian soprano with an impressive set of lungs.

I managed to wiggle my way inside without dropping anything, a feat I was probably more proud of than was justified by the situation. Then I turned toward the counters to deposit everything safely.

"Martha? Are you here? I'm ba—"

My bags crashed to the floor.

Martha lay slumped across the kitchen table.

An apron was tied around her neck.

CHAPTER
SEVEN

"Martha!" Racing across the room, I pulled her over, tearing frantically at the apron. One of my nails broke. I didn't slow down.

If I could get it off, maybe she'd be okay. Maybe this just happened. Maybe—

"Emma." Pink's voice barely penetrated the panic in my mind. "She's gone."

Lying Martha gently on her back, I realized he was right. Her eyes were wide up, staring at the ceiling with no sight. She was way beyond chest compressions. I did them, anyway.

My hands kept moving to the beat of "Staying Alive" until a spot of blood dripped onto Martha's chest. With a start, I realized it was mine. The pink apron had been knotted so firmly, I shredded my fingers trying to rip it off. Until seeing the evidence, I hadn't even felt the pain.

"How could this happen?" I asked frantically. "I need scissors. Where are the scissors?"

This was a kitchen. Every kitchen had shears somewhere. But where?

"You need to call the police."

"Go find Josie. Make sure she doesn't come in here."

He took off through the swinging door. I patted my pockets several times before finally realizing my phone wasn't in them. Either it fell out or I'd forgotten to grab it before leaving for my walk. Thank goodness I'd had the landline installed. We had an extension in the foyer and one in here.

It didn't take long to get through to the emergency number.

The dispatcher assured me an officer would be here as soon as possible. The police department in Willow Falls wasn't large, and they rarely dealt with murder, so we were their number one priority.

"Do you want me to stay on the phone with you until they arrive?" she asked.

"I don't think so. I need to make sure everyone is okay."

"Are you alone in the house?"

"No. It's a B&B. There is someone else here, but I'm not sure where she is at the moment."

The dispatcher started to say something. It sounded like a warning, so I hung up. She wasn't going to convince me not to check on Josie's welfare. What if her ex-husband had found us? She might be in the same condition as Martha.

Pink bounded back through the door as I hung up.

"Josie is in her room. She doesn't appear to be injured. I did a quick circle of the house, and I don't believe there's anyone else on the premises. Whoever did this is gone."

Okay, great.

Should I untie the apron? No. Probably a bad idea.

Should I sit down?

Stand?

Pace?

Having never found a dead body before, I didn't have the first clue what I to do. I suspected I might be in shock. How did people treat shock? No idea. It seemed like blankets might be involved. This wasn't helpful. Maybe I should google the signs of shock. I needed my phone. I needed to calm down.

"Did you see who did this?" I asked Pink.

"No. I walked in right before you did."

My head spun. Moving into the foyer, I checked the driveway. The only cars there were mine and Martha's—same as when I got back from the farmers market. No surprise.

Should I wait here for the police to arrive?

Since Pink and I had concluded no one else was in immediate danger, I went back into the kitchen. As weird as it sounded, I didn't want Martha to be alone. We'd barely known each other, sure, and our last interaction hadn't exactly been positive, but she'd been killed in my house. Part of me felt responsible. I should be able to protect my employees. Security cameras, magic spells, whatever it took.

"...appy.... ooo.... ou...."

A voice stopped me in my tracks. I cocked my head, listening.

It didn't sound like a television. Also, the TV in the living area hung on the wall about fifteen feet away. The dark screen was plainly visible from my vantage point. Someone else was in the house!

The thought sent a chill down my spine. Pull it together, Emma. Time to investigate.

At first I thought the voice was coming from upstairs. After I'd made it up three or four steps, I realized the sound was now behind me. Coming from the ballroom of all places. Other than walking through it when showing Cliff around, I'd barely set foot in there the past few days. Had he come back to start the work we'd talked about?

No, Cliff's voice wasn't quite as deep as this one. Besides, he didn't seem to be the "walk around singing while you work" type.

Nope. It wasn't a person at all. Well, not a live one. The ballroom was Walter's domain.

More importantly, I had a magic cat. "Pink, who's in there?"

"How should I know?"

"You're stealthy. Go look. Is it Walter? Last time I saw him, he was outside on the porch. He didn't come in with me."

I swear that cat smirked at me. "You know, I may be your familiar, but I'm not your employee. If you want to know who is in there, I suggest you go look."

It was probably my grandfather making that noise. Then again, it didn't hurt to be cautious when there was a killer on the loose. Although the cat wasn't exactly a body-guard, staying near him made me feel better.

"You wouldn't send me to my death, would you? Remember who feeds you."

The singing continued, and I realized that the tune sounded familiar, although the thick double doors obscured the words. "Maybe if you bought better food, I'd help."

Okay, then. Either it was Walter in there, or my cat was out to get me.

The police were on their way. I'd be fine.

Taking a deep breath, I eased the ballroom door open. Thank goodness for well-magicked—er, oiled—hinges.

Then I slipped inside, careful not to make any noise, just in case I was wrong about the singer's identity.

In the middle of the dance floor, wearing a huge smile and a party hat, was Walter. He'd spread his arms wide and was belting out a tune while facing the ceiling.

"Happy Death Day, My Deeeaaaar Friend! Happy Death Day toooooooo yoooooooouuuuuuu!"

Walter, was apparently, utterly delighted not to be the only deceased person in the house.

Although I would've sworn I didn't make a sound, he spun toward me. "Emma! Isn't this exciting?"

Before I could tell him that his song was in appallingly bad taste, another apparition shimmered into view.

"Excuse me." To my utter shock, Martha now stood before me. She still wore her chef's jacket, hair pulled back in that eyebrow-aching bun. But now she was also translucent. I could see Walter through her, and on the far side of the room, the glass double doors leading to the patio. "Can someone please explain what happened to me? I appear to have lost my body, and I don't like it one bit!"

Walter tilted his head at the second ghost to arrive. "That's why I'm here. Listen, I'll show you the ropes."

She screamed. "A ghost! There's a ghost! My heart... Why isn't my heart pounding?"

"I'm sorry to tell you this, but I think you're dead." I tried to sound as sympathetic as possible, as if I wasn't praying she'd actually slipped some hallucinogens into yesterday's eggs and I'd wake up safely in my bed any second. This was so surreal, part of me expected to wake up any moment and find myself dreaming.

"Dead? I most certainly am not!" She put her hands on her hips. "I demand you tell me the truth immediately, or I'll call the police."

"Why don't you try it, Toots?" Walter asked.

I couldn't tell if he was trying to sound like a member of the cast of *The Godfather*, but his attitude wasn't helpful. I stepped between the ghosts and put my hands up, as if that would do any good. Surprisingly, they both backed up. "Calm down, everyone. Martha, the police are on the way. Walter, did you, by any chance, see what happened?"

"Of course I did! What, you think there's a body in my home right under my nose and I don't know about it? I'm insulted. Remember, I'm the one who told you to get in there?"

Considering that was exactly what just happened to me, actually, yes, I did. But it didn't seem worth bringing that up. Especially when I realized Josie was in her bedroom, only about fifteen feet down the hallway. At any moment, she might hear voices and come looking for me. The police were also on their way. I didn't want any of them to find me talking to a pair of ghosts.

I needed to redirect this conversation quickly. "What happened?"

"Isn't it obvious?" He gave me a withering look. "Someone *killed* Martha. Don't tell me you thought it was an accident. Vera was so smart. She'd be devastated not to have passed that on."

Taking a deep breath, I forced myself to exhale before responding. "I meant, who killed her?"

"How should I know?"

"You said you see everything here! I asked you not three seconds ago, and you said, 'you think there's a body in my home right under my nose and I don't know about it? I'm insulted.'" My Walter impression wasn't spot on, but it was close enough to drive the point home.

"Excuse me." Martha stood with her hands folded

primly together as if waiting for her dinner reservation. "Can you two do this without me?"

"I'm sorry," I said. "Yes, of course. I'm supposed to help you move on. I think. Before I got my magic, I couldn't see ghosts, so I'm not entirely sure. Do you have any unfinished business that needs to be resolved?"

Ignoring me, she turned her steely gaze on Walter. "Are you a ghost, too? Can you explain how this works?"

"Yes, ma'am. I'm not a spirit guide, though. I've had no one but a cat to talk to for the last twenty-six years." When I glared at him, he added, "But of course, I'll help you if I can."

"Excellent. Thank you," she said. "Where's the light? I'd like to go into it, please."

"That's it?" Not that I needed a hysterical ghost on my hands but she seemed awfully calm. "You're not upset? You don't want to know how you died or who was responsible?"

"Would getting upset make me not dead?"

"No, I don't think it works like that."

"Then what's the point?" She shook her head. "My Rodney died twenty years ago, when our youngest was a toddler. Now that I see there is life after death, I'd like to become reacquainted. I've missed him terribly. Where should I go?"

As if summoned by her words, a shimmering door appeared behind her. The knob glowed.

"Right through there," Walter said with a flourish.

She looked at me. "I'm sorry to leave you, and during my very first shift. I've never called in sick a day in my life. But I'm in no condition to work for you."

"I don't blame you at all," I assured her. "I don't think ghosts can cook, if it helps."

"I can cook!" Walter said loudly. "You just can't eat my food."

We ignored him.

"Excellent. Well then, please tell my grandchildren I love them." Martha took a step toward the door, then stopped and turn back to me. "Wait. My daughter-in-law. Can you tell her that my cinnamon roll recipe is hidden inside my jewelry box? She's been asking for years. I know she always thought I didn't like her because I refused to give away my secret ingredient. But she's good for my boy, and I want her to have it now. Bottom drawer. It's locked, but the key is in an old bottle of expired medicine in my bathroom. No one would ever go in there."

"Absolutely," I said.

"Thank you. Goodbye."

She opened the door. On the other side stood a guy who looked like he was in his mid-twenties. He wore military fatigues and a look of pure love. A tear formed in Martha's eye, and her face widened into the first smile I'd seen. She opened her arms and stepped forward. When she passed through the doorway, they both shimmered out of sight. The door vanished a second later.

"Well, that was unexpected," I said. "Imagine getting murdered and not caring who did it."

"She had a point." He shrugged. "The answer wouldn't change anything, would it? She'd still be dead."

"It would make me feel better," I grumbled, knowing very well this wasn't about me. "You really didn't see anything?"

He shook his head. "Sorry. I saw the body, heard you walking on the porch, and told you to go inside. That's it."

"You didn't see anyone in the house?"

"No one but you and Josie."

Darn it. This could have been resolved so easily. "Where were you when it happened?"

"In here." Walter gestured around himself. "I'm in here most of the time. Great light, lots of memories."

"Who are you talking to?"

A voice in the doorway made me jump. Behind me, Josie stood in the doorway wearing a set of clothes I'd given her and looking more relaxed than the last time we spoke. Hopefully some time alone helped her calm down. Her hands were on her hips, head tilted to one side.

Somehow I knew that "talking to my ghostly guests" wasn't the right answer. Good thing because as I twisted my whole body around to face her, I realized Walter had also disappeared.

Not that she would have been able to see him.

"Testing the acoustics" would be a great answer any time other than immediately after finding a dead body.

For too long, I hesitated. Josie was, to my knowledge, the only other person who'd been in the house all morning. The most logical conclusion was that she had been the one to kill Martha, especially after their argument this morning. But I didn't want to believe she could be a killer.

We'd connected instantly. Similar age, both with pasts we preferred not to talk about. She was afraid of something, and I didn't think it was Martha.

She was still looking at me, waiting for an answer. If I didn't say something soon, it would just keep getting more awkward.

Finally, I opted for a partial truth. "Um, this room makes me feel closer to my grandfather. When I get scared or flustered, I come in here and talk to him as if he can hear me. I know it's weird but listen—"

"No weirder than any other coping mechanism," she said. "What's wrong?"

Right, she didn't know yet. Not like Pink could have told her. There was no way to sugarcoat this. "Martha's dead. I'm waiting for the police."

She blinked several times, but that was her only reaction. "Excuse me?"

"After you went back to your room, I went upstairs to shower. Then I decided to go to the farmers market to get breakfast. Martha could bake whatever she wanted, but she was so upset, and I wasn't positive she'd be back. If I made something myself, I'd just poison you so—"

"Emma?"

Her quiet interruption stopped me. "I'm rambling, aren't I?"

"A little. Take a deep breath."

"When I came back, I found her slumped over the kitchen table. It looked like she'd been rolling out the dough for the famous cinnamon rolls she was talking about. She..." My eyes filled with tears. "Someone had strangled her."

Josie gasped. "When you said she died, I thought you meant it was a heart attack. How terrible!"

"It really was. Did you see anyone after leaving the kitchen this morning?"

"Not a soul. Martha made such a big deal about me being in her space, I hid. I was in my room until about two minutes ago. My stomach growled, and I could see Martha's car from the porch, so I knew she'd come back. I figured I should make amends if I ever wanted to eat again. Then I heard you in here, talking to yourself. I stopped to see if you wanted to go with me."

"Why?"

Her cheeks turned pink. "I thought our conversation might go better if we had an intermediary."

For the first time, I became very aware that, as the only other person in the house, Josie had the perfect opportunity to kill Martha while I was out. No. I couldn't believe that. "Maybe if I'd been a better go-between earlier, she wouldn't have been alone in the kitchen when she died."

"If she'd been alone, she'd still be alive. The question is, who was with her?"

CHAPTER
EIGHT

S till a little disoriented from the events of the last half hour, I moved back to the entryway to wait for the police to arrive and also to waylay any unsuspecting travelers who might show up. The last thing I wanted was for someone else to wander in off the street to rent a room and stumble onto Martha's body. Josie headed down the hall toward her room.

To my surprise, a sturdy man with graying brown hair stood inside the double doors, examining the front desk. There was this confident air about him, giving off a Pierce-Brosnan-as-James-Bond vibe. He wasn't as tall, but the self-assurance came off him in waves.

It had been a long morning. If this guy was a Crown spy, he needed to come back later.

"Good morning," I said. "I'm Emma. I'm afraid we're closed due to a... staffing issue. Can you come back in a few hours?"

"Staffing issue? That's a good one." His lips twitched. "I'm Detective Timothy Pratt with the Willow Falls PD."

That gave me pause. He wasn't wearing a badge, and he looked younger than the cops I'd seen on TV. Then again, I hadn't watched television in a long time, and I wasn't exactly a spring chicken anymore. My dentist looked about twelve.

"Oh." I blinked at him. Not an assassin. Cop. "So you don't need a place to stay, then. Sorry. You look so tired."

The words were out of my mouth before I realized how they sounded. If only my magic let me rewind five seconds at a time, I would rock my social interactions.

"No. Glad to hear you think I'm so very pretty, though." My cheeks grew warm, but then he smiled. "Relax, I'm kidding. The dispatcher said you found the body in the kitchen, so my men are already in there processing the crime scene. I was waiting to talk to you. I have a few questions, then I'm headed home. Normally I look much better, but I'm coming off an all-nighter. Your place was on my way, so they called me."

"I feel like I should apologize for delaying your sleep."

"Not at all," he said. "Where were you just now?"

"In the ballroom. The space calms me."

"Right. Anyone else on the property?"

"Just Josie. She works here." And my grandfather's ghost and his suspiciously old talking cat.

"Okay. I'll need to talk to her, too. Is there a place where we can sit down while we chat?"

"Yes, of course. I'm sorry. Right this way." Two uniformed officers were working in the kitchen, so I led him into the dining area. I didn't know if they'd taken Martha's body out yet, but I'd prefer to wait until someone told me they were done. "The coffee maker is in the kitchen, or I'd offer you some."

"That's quite all right." He settled into a table on the

edge of the room, facing the door. I took the seat across from him.

While Detective Pratt pulled a notebook out of his breast pocket and flipped through the pages, I examined him. Up close, he looked less like James Bond, but still good-looking. The hint of crow's feet at his eyes made him look wise, and he had a kind face.

I just hoped he was smart and efficient. There was a killer on the loose, and I'd feel much better once someone caught them. Even with magical protections, the thought of sleeping in this big house mostly alone freaked me out.

As soon as we got settled, Pink bounded through the cat door and hopped onto my lap. A stray leaf from the garden stuck in his whiskers. "Don't say anything stupid. You have a right to remain silent, you know."

Like I was a suspect.

That thought stopped me in my tracks.

Was I a suspect? I'd found the body, I'd called it in, but that didn't exactly exonerate me. Sure, I didn't have a motive, but Detective Pratt couldn't possibly know that. We hadn't even started talking yet. I had the opportunity and an alibi that only worked if they could narrow her death to the five-minute window when I was talking to Beth out of the entire time I was alone this morning. Something told me science wasn't quite that advanced yet.

Since I couldn't respond to Pink verbally, I petted him absently, pulling the leaf out. When he sniffed my face, then rubbed his nose along my cheek, I relaxed. Cat magic or actual? Sometimes, it didn't matter.

"Beautiful cat," Detective Pratt said.

At that, Pink puffed out his chest with pride. Cheeky little thing.

"He certainly thinks so," I replied.

"Heh. Do you mind, though? It's better if you're not distracted while we're talking."

He had no idea how distracting this particular feline could be. Without me even having to ask, Pink hopped down. The brandish of his hind quarters told Detective Pratt how he felt about being sent away. He sauntered over to the next table and hopped on a chair before settling down, eyes still fixed on us.

"What's your full name?"

"Emma Faden."

"The deceased woman's name is Martha Armstrong. She worked here, is that right?"

"Yes." Before she vanished permanently, police officers used to come looking for my mom from time to time. When someone told them what they wanted to know, she tended to disappear for at least a few days. An entire year once. As a result, I'd learned not to volunteer more information than asked.

"Are you the one who hired her?"

"Yes."

"Are you the sole owner of this property?"

"Yes, I am."

"Geez, lady."

I smiled at him innocently.

His eyes pleaded with me. "Please help me out here. It's been a long night, getting longer by the second. You're not in any trouble. I just need to know what happened. You don't want someone dangerous hanging around your B&B, do you? That won't be good for business. Until we get this solved, everyone is a suspect. We just need to narrow down the possibilities. Talk to everyone who has been here."

My heart went out to the guy. It wasn't his fault I was like this, and he was only doing his job. He didn't seem like the jerk cops I'd dealt with in the past. Also, as an adult, I had started to suspect my mother's legal problems were more her fault than the state's.

Detective Pratt looked like he'd be better off tucked away in one of the rooms upstairs than sitting across from me asking questions. If I wanted to further my life's calling of helping people, I should start with him. Not to mention helping get justice for Martha.

Taking it moment by moment, I told him what happened from the time I left the B&B until I came back in through the kitchen door. He took notes the whole time.

When I finished, he tapped something into his phone before looking at me. "Okay, thanks. How many total applicants were there for the job?"

"Two."

"Do you know how I can reach the other?"

"Josie is still here. Her cooking sucked, but she needed a job and a place to stay. I'm giving her a chance at the front desk. Her number is in my phone, which I haven't seen since before I left for the farmers market. It's probably either on the front desk or upstairs. But her room is down the hall."

I didn't mention the front desk really didn't need anyone to operate it, since it would tell me when anyone came in.

"You gave her a different job than the one she applied for, just because she needed it? That was awfully nice of you."

His expression suggested he wasn't buying my story, even though it was true. Part of me didn't blame him—as a detective, even in a small town like this, Detective Pratt had a front seat to some of humanity's worst traits. He probably wasn't used to someone helping a stranger with no ulterior motive.

"Thanks. I figure there's no sense in me having this giant house and all the money that came with it unless I'm going to help people." The story of my inheritance had been major news, so there was no point pretending my fortune didn't exist. I sensed Detective Pratt would appreciate me acknowledging the money.

The connecting door to the kitchen swung open, and a short, stocky officer with spiky black hair appeared. His name tag identified him as S. Gutierrez. He carried a plastic bag in his hands. It wasn't until he got to the table that I realized what was in it. "Do you recognize this, ma'am?"

"Emma, please. Ma'am makes me feel old enough to be your mother." My cheeks grew warm when I realized that S. Gutierrez probably hadn't had his twenty-fifth birthday yet. I *was* old enough to be his mother.

Detective Pratt cleared his throat and pointed at the bag. "Emma, have you seen this before?"

The hot pink color shone through the plastic like a beacon. "That's the apron, isn't it? I found it tied around Martha's throat."

"Had you ever seen it before you found her?"

I nodded. "I bought several aprons last week in a variety of colors. Hung them on hooks in the kitchen. There's an entire row by the door. I'm pretty sure this was one of them."

"Has anyone worn it since you bought it?"

"I did," I said. "Josie put it on yesterday when she interviewed for the cook position. But it was hanging right inside the door where anyone could have—"

"We understand that," Detective Pratt said. "Thanks, Gutierrez."

He paused, watching until the officer had gone back into the kitchen. The apron went with him, and I felt a bit of relief at getting it out of my sight.

Pink said, "If Josie killed Martha, you don't want to get caught making excuses for her."

"I don't think she did it!" I said hotly.

Luckily, Detective Pratt thought I was talking to him. "That's what we're here to find out. Was anything taken from the kitchen?"

Shaking my head to clear it, I closed my eyes and focused on the scene. Most of the items of value in the kitchen were attached to the building: the wrought iron chef's rack hanging above the island. The gorgeous copper farmhouse sink. The dual ovens. The fridge.

"I don't know. I didn't get a chance to look. But it was all pots and pans... is the KitchenAid still on the counter by the fridge?"

"The giant mixer? Yeah, it's there," he said. "Call me if you notice anything missing. We're guessing this wasn't a robbery. The victim's purse was on a shelf in the walk-in pantry. That would usually be the first thing someone would grab. Certainly before walking off with a twenty-pound mixer."

"Right. Thanks. I'll keep you posted."

"Did anything unusual happen this morning? Anyone here who wasn't supposed to be? Martha say anything about someone who was mad at her? Did she have an argument with either of you?"

Oh. I didn't want to answer that, but I didn't have a choice. If I lied and Josie told him about the argument, my covering for her would look bad. Also, Pink was glaring at me so hard, I wondered if he was trying to force me to spill the details with some kind of cat mind control.

Not wanting to see how he would react if I lied, I told a carefully constructed truth. "This morning when I was upstairs in my room, I heard raised voices. It sounded like two people were arguing. I didn't catch most of what they were saying."

Detective Pratt let out a "hmmm" and made a note on his pad. I couldn't read it. "Sound travels that far in this house?"

"My windows were open. The kitchen is directly below me. Either they were standing in the garden or their windows were also open. They were inside when I came down the stairs." It hadn't occurred to me to check whether the windows were open when I found Martha.

"Dirt on the kitchen floor," he muttered, mostly to himself. "That tracks. Did many people use the kitchen entrance?"

"Only three of us are here. I used that door when I came back from the farmers market," I said. "The footprints might be mine. Otherwise, the only person who would have a reason to use that door was Martha. Or a delivery person."

"Have you had any deliveries recently?"

I shook my head. "Martha mentioned wanting to place an order this morning. I don't know if she got the chance."

"You said you were sleeping when she had the argument. When did you talk to her?"

"She arrived for her shift at four-thirty this morning. Something about needing time to prepare fresh cinnamon rolls. I let her in, gave her a key for next time, told her to order whatever she needed, and stumbled back to bed."

"Why didn't she already have a key?"

"It was her first day. I hired her over the phone yesterday. It didn't make sense for her to come back just for the key when I would be here to let her in."

"How did this other woman, this Josie, take it when you told her she couldn't have the job?"

"Fine," I said. "She was thrilled that I offered her a different position. She is not a good cook. The idea of Josie killing Martha to get my chef job makes about as much sense as me killing you so I can be a detective."

He chuckled. "I'll watch my back. Wait a sec, Josie Ross?"

"Yeah, why?"

"She's an excellent cook. She caters the church barbecue every summer. No matter how much we buy, the brisket always runs out. Fights have broken out in line over people cutting. She's that good."

Confusion wrinkled my brow. The dish Josie had presented me was practically inedible. If a well-qualified cook botched an interview for a job, would she kill the person who won it over her? I didn't want to believe it. But this added information gave me pause. What went wrong? She'd been rattled by seeing Martha. So much that she couldn't prepare a meal? Something wasn't right.

Pratt must have noticed the change in my expression. "Is there anything else you want to tell me? Anything at all that might be helpful?"

Having known Martha for less than twenty-four hours, it was extremely difficult to guess who might want to kill her. Sure, she hadn't exactly had a warm and fuzzy demeanor, but a person's personality didn't justify murder.

Baked goods. Something prickled at the back of my mind.

"The farmers market!"

He tilted his head at me. "What about it?"

"When I was there this morning, one of the vendors told me her sister had an argument with Martha. Something about pastries." I shook my head. "Sorry, I don't remember the details. The sister wasn't there, so I didn't get to ask her about it."

"When was this?"

"About fifteen minutes before I found Martha, probably. I finished shopping and walked back, so however long that takes. I wasn't in a hurry. Then I walked in, saw what happened, and called the police a couple of minutes later."

"A couple of minutes? Why did you wait?"

My cheeks flushed. "I panicked. Couldn't think what to do. Tried CPR, tried to take off the apron—incidentally, I may have bled on her chest while doing compressions."

That couldn't look good. But better to disclose now than have him find out from the lab later.

"You got your blood on the victim?"

"Not on purpose! I was trying to save her life. Then, when I realized that wasn't possible, I went looking for my phone. That's when I called you."

He made a note. "In the future, if you could avoid contaminating any evidence you should come across, I'd appreciate it."

"Again, I'm very sorry." A thought occurred to me. "Martha has a key to this house. Was it in her purse?"

"We'll check. You might want to consider changing the locks, just to be safe. But Emma?"

"Yeah?"

"This is a crime scene." He gestured around him. "Not just the kitchen. The whole house. Really, we should have made you wait outside while we were gathering evidence. I'll speak with Officer Gutierrez later. But this death involves foul play, which means we need to preserve the area."

"What are you saying?"

"You're going to have to shut down for the duration. Is there somewhere you can go for about a week or so? A friend you can stay with?"

I gaped at him. "We just opened for business today!"

"I know, and I'm sorry," he said. "But my hands are tied. If we want to bring Martha's killer to justice, we need the entire mansion to be secured and empty while we investigate. You can take a bag, but that's it."

"A bag and my cat, right?"

"Well, yes. Please take the cat."

"I don't like his tone," Pink said. "He says 'cat' as if I'm some kind of inferior being."

Ignoring him, I said, "I just moved to town. I don't have anyone to stay with."

"No family? There's another bed-and-breakfast nearby."

As if I'd give Toby the pleasure of checking into his competing business after the way he spoken to me. Not even if every other establishment in Willow Falls caught fire. I'd go back to sleeping in my Toyota. "There are some outbuildings in the back. Guest houses. No one has been in there since I moved in. Can I stay in one of them?"

"I'll send a couple of officers back after we finish up, make sure they're clear. For all you know, there's a killer hiding in your pool house."

A chill went down my spine. "An excellent point. I'll wait for the okay."

"Thanks. Now, where can I find Josie?"

I nodded toward the doorway. "She's down the hall. If you don't need anything else, I'll go get her."

After Detective Pratt released me, I headed down the hall toward Josie's room. The poor woman must be terrified. She seemed so meek to me, practically afraid of her own shadow. Wouldn't harm a fly. This had to be all a big misunderstanding. They argued, Josie walked away, someone else came in from outside (leaving dirt on the floors!) and killed Martha.

It was almost as implausible as the "different car" theory in *My Cousin Vinny*, and yet, I held onto it.

I knocked on Josie's door. No answer.

After counting out thirty seconds, I knocked again. This time when she didn't respond, I called her name. Nothing.

Although my every instinct screamed against it, I twisted the knob and opened the door a crack. If I didn't take Josie to Detective Pratt, he'd come back with a warrant. That would make everything worse. "Josie? Are you in there?"

When only silence hit my ears, I pushed the door open further. "If you're here, it's better to come with me than to wait for the police to come get you."

Inside the room, chaos reigned. Drawers pulled open and emptied. The closet door stood wide, with nothing but empty hangers inside. The sheets on the bed were rumpled. I poked around, but couldn't find a suitcase anywhere.

Josie was gone.

NINE

Even I had to admit this looked bad. To be honest, I didn't want to tell Detective Pratt that Josie had run away, but there really wasn't any way around it. To delay the inevitable, I went to the porch to check her parking spot. Maybe she'd gone for a walk...with all her belongings? I know, I know.

As expected, her car was gone.

Detective Pratt must have been watching through the windows, because the front door opened and he stepped out onto the porch.

"What's wrong?"

As badly as I didn't want to throw my friend under the bus, my options were limited. "Josie's not in her room. I don't know where she went."

No reason to mention that all her stuff was gone.

"Is that her car?" He pointed at a dark blue Nissan sedan in the driveway. "Does it belong to a guest?"

"That's Martha's car. Josie was parked on the other side, over by her room."

He copied the plate number, then handed me a business card. "Thanks for your help. I'll be in touch. Please let me know if you think of anything. When your friend comes back, let her know I'd like to ask some questions about anything she observed. Meanwhile, Officer Gutierrez will escort you to your room so you can pack some things."

Wonderful.

With the officer by my side, I went up the stairs and put my suitcase on the trunk at the foot of the bed. Officer Gutierrez moved into my bathroom, checked the shower and the closet, peeked under the bed—as if a full-sized person would fit!—then went to stand in the doorway. Pink waited at his feet.

Once all my clothes were packed, I went into the attached bathroom. Besides the normal daily stuff, I grabbed a spare set of sheets and towels from the linen closet, then my pillow from the bed. I didn't have any idea how well stocked the outbuildings were. I might be sleeping on a wooden floor in an entirely empty room. Until I conjured up a bed.

Then I glanced at my trunk and hesitated. It wasn't just for looks—the heavily spelled container held the books Walter had left me, which could be useful. I could study and practice my magic. Learn some new spells, maybe find something to help identify Martha's killer. Then I could return home.

I'd only been here a few weeks, but after a lifetime of feeling like I didn't belong anywhere, I wasn't excited about leaving the one place where I felt content. Not to mention, it was hard to use a mansion to help people who needed a place to stay if they had to sleep in the driveway.

A meow drew my attention to the doorway.

"If you want your spell books, grab them now," Pink said. "I've got him."

Surprised, I glanced from my cat to Officer Gutierrez. He still stood in the opening, eyes closed. Still as a statue. Pink leaning against his calves.

"Tell me you didn't put the whammy on a police officer." That couldn't be legal.

"He'll be fine. He won't even know he missed anything. But you've got about thirty seconds, so let's not waste it."

At that, I flew into action. I yanked the trunk open, grabbed Walter's spell book and my own mostly empty Lisa Frank notebook, then closed the lid as quietly as possible. We couldn't have a second officer coming up to ask what was thumping around up here.

My bedroom suite was heavily protected. The doorway at the bottom of the stairs was spelled to make people forget where they were going the second they stepped through unless they were with me. They should immediately get an overwhelming urge to leave. Officer Gutierrez made it up beside me, but if Detective Pratt tried to investigate, he'd have a lot of unanswerable questions. With that in mind, the books went into my suitcase in the blink of an eye.

As I was zipping it shut, Officer Gutierrez sneezed three times.

"Bless you," I said.

"Thanks. Sorry about that."

"It's okay. There's a lot of dust up here. Shall we?"

"Just a sec." For a minute, I worried he was going to ask what happened to him. Instead, he pulled out a walkie-talkie, turned his back to me, and radioed someone. Most of their conversation was too quiet and crackly for me to follow, but when he finished, he said, "We're all clear. The lower floors are secure. I'm to escort you out of the building and wait for you to lock up."

Wonderful.

"Any sign of Josie?" I asked. "I don't have her cell phone number, so I can't tell her to stay out."

"We haven't found anyone on the grounds," he said. "The police tape should be a hint, though. Don't forget to call when if comes back."

I sighed. "I know."

Although it pained me to think about betraying someone who trusted me, I was at heart a rule follower. If Josie really attacked Martha, she needed to be brought to justice. Otherwise, eliminating her as a suspect might help them figure out who did it. If they were focused on the wrong person, they might never find Martha's killer. Either way, protecting her was probably not going to help find the murderer any faster.

Officer Gutierrez led me down the stairs while I tried to think of a way to ask Pink to notify my ghost that I'd be moving out for a few days. He took off around the time the police arrived, and I hadn't seen him since. Walter had been so excited when I'd first arrived at the mansion, he'd be devastated if I vanished with no explanation. But the cat had taken off for parts unknown, as he frequently did. He could be anywhere by now, from sleeping in the hayloft in the barn to chasing mice out by the forest. I was starting to suspect that his repertoire included teleporting.

I'd have to find come back in to speak with Walter later. This place had a lot of doors and windows. The police couldn't block all of them, could they?

Outside, I surveyed the various outbuildings before

choosing one. Nearest to the house was an old stable that had been converted into a garage about fifty years ago. I would probably park there come winter, but I hadn't gotten around to repairing the door yet. The inside needed a good purging and deep clean before it was remotely usable. That had been my next magical project when Dottie arrived and gave me the warning, so I'd put it on my "Worry About Later" list.

Behind the stable, we had an old pool house, which held equipment to clean the (empty, drained, and very cracked) swimming pool. Although it was a rather hot August this year, that hadn't been a priority, either. I kept forgetting I had money now and could pay people to do things like fix my pool.

If I recalled correctly, the pool house was crammed full of old deck furniture that mostly needed to be repaired or replaced. The small cottage had been intended for people to change—there was a bathroom, but I didn't think it even had a shower. Yellow police tape ringed it. I didn't ask why, because they probably wouldn't tell me. Either way, that was out.

To my left, there were two smaller cottages that the lawyer had told me used to be servant housing. They hadn't been used for anything as long as Frank remembered. As far as I knew, they looked more or less the same inside: one bedroom, a small living area with an attached kitchenette. Not much space to cook, which was fine. As long as the takeout people could find me, I'd be happy. The only other thing worth noticing was a functional, non-exciting full bathroom.

I pointed. "Have those been checked and determined safe?"

He nodded. "You can enter any building that doesn't

have the police tape. We're doing the main house now. I checked those cottages myself. Personally, I'd go with the one in the back. The front one looks like it would require more work to make livable."

Livable. Right. Ugh.

I needed to clean a cottage and get all the things that would make it nice enough to stay for a few days, and I wasn't even supposed to use my magic. The minor spells I'd risked here and there appeared to have gone unnoticed (or at least been discrete enough to be okay), but a full deep cleaning was the kind of flashy magic that got me into trouble.

After thanking the officer, I went to the building he'd indicated and pushed the front door open. The unit was cozy. Ahead of me was a perfectly serviceable kitchen, considering I didn't know how to cook. I had a stove, a sink, and a fridge. No dishwasher, but what did you expect in a tiny place built before electricity existed? I could buy a few things to heat in the oven or grab a microwave at the local superstore and be fine as far as food went.

To the right was the living area. Dusty, but not terrible. Walter's housekeeper must have come out here while he was still alive, because there was an overstuffed couch covered by a drop cloth, an old school entertainment center like the one my parents had when I was in high school, and a massive TV from the 1990s. The store would have a better one of those, too. Something that didn't weigh forty pounds.

After carefully removing the dust cloth from the sofa, I walked around, opening all the windows to air the place out. Then I wheeled my suitcase into the bedroom. More of the same: a thin coating of dust everywhere. A wooden dresser, a small closet with no hangers, a double bed also covered in dusty sheets. I grabbed those, too, although I had no idea where to find a washer/dryer without going back into the mansion. Maybe the pool house had one for towels.

In a room attached to the living area, I found a small but functional bathroom with a shower. A door beside the pantry, to my surprise, led down to a small basement. It seemed odd for an outbuilding, but this place was built hundreds of years ago. Maybe this one was originally used for cold storage.

After Pink helpfully assured me that no murderer lurked down there, I went to check for myself. Nothing but spider webs. Whatever the basement's original purpose, it hadn't been used for quite some time.

Unfortunately, it wasn't used to store cleaning supplies. No vacuum, broom, dustpan, mop, or bucket anywhere in the house. Not even a sponge for the kitchen sink.

Like it or not, I was going to have to go shopping. I couldn't wait for the things I needed to be delivered. Unless, maybe... I could do a basic cleaning spell, now? Something little. Totally unnoticeable. I mulled the possibilities while climbing back up the stairs.

Hands on my hips, I surveyed the bedroom. I wanted to fix it so badly, my mouth was practically watering. My fingers twitched at the thought of getting to snap a spell into existence.

"You know, one tiny incantation would make this place shine," I said to Pink. "I wouldn't even need to buy a mop."

"Doing magic when this place is crawling with humans?" he asked. "What if one of the police officers comes back to find you in a sparkling clean cottage after leaving you in a musty, old dump? Dottie was pretty clear when she spoke to you."

"Why can you do magic when I can't?"

"Because I understand necessity and moderation." He raised one paw. "Before you say anything, yes, getting Walter's book was a necessity."

I wasn't going to argue that point. Having the spell book helped me significantly, if only because I wouldn't have to break in to get it against police orders. "Fine, we'll go to the store."

Pink meowed.

"What?" I asked.

"You, um, can't use magic to change the furniture, upgrade the appliances, or paint the walls. But you could save time cleaning up the bedroom and unpacking."

My hands went to my hips. "What are you talking about?"

"Ambient magic. It's inherently found in things—common types are plant magic, weather magic, food magic... and thread magic."

"I have thread magic! You're saying it can't be traced?"

"Ambient magic is subtle. It comes from the thing being manipulated instead of the person. When you changed the entire exterior of the house after you arrived, that was elemental magic. It comes from your inherent power—which was inherited from your grandfather. Your grandmother, like you, had ambient magic. Isn't that why you have her name?"

"What are you talking about?" I asked him.

"Your last name. Faden."

"Yeah? I think it's German."

"Yes, it is," Pink said smugly. "It's German for thread. Your grandmother was a thread witch. She must not have taken her husband's name."

I thought for a moment. "He took hers. I don't remember why."

"I could guess," Pink said. "Regardless, the spells where your clothes don't wrinkle and the sheets don't get dirty? Those are ambient."

I started to thank him, then paused. "Why didn't you mention this earlier?"

"You weren't ready yet," he said. "I'm not sure you're ready now, but we've got little to do but practice, so we might as well talk about it. See if you can lift the dusty sheet and fold it without making a mess."

Closing my eyes, I reached for my power. Although it flowed through my veins, I thought of it sitting inside my chest, like a spool of thread. There it was. Tentatively, I touched it to see how it felt. It shimmered.

Teasing out a thread of magic, I tossed it onto the bed. Then I raised my hands up, directing the sheet to move upward.

"You don't need to be showy about it," Pink grumbled.

"Hush. I'm just getting the hang of things."

The sheet was filthy, so once I had it up in the air, I lifted each corner carefully. When the middle sagged, I connected the far right and near left corners. To my utter joy, it worked! As I focused, the remaining two corners also met, creating a packet. At my direction, the whole thing moved and rotated in the air, folding over and over. Finally, I asked it to drop into my hands. Looking down, I realized that I held a perfectly folded square with not a speck of dust on the outside.

A squeal of delight escaped me.

"That was amazing!" I said.

"Not bad for a beginner."

"From you, I'll consider that high praise."

"As you should."

"If only I could do the same with mops and brooms..." I tapped one finger to my lips, imagining the possibilities.

"Maybe one day. Also, they're back in the main house. You need to go to the store for cleaning supplies. And, more importantly, cat food."

"Thanks for reminding me," I grumbled.

Food.

"Why aren't you moving?" Pink asked.

"Because the police have shut my bed-and-breakfast down, and I have guests expected over the next few days. I'm going to have to call everyone and cancel."

"They can wait."

I shook my head. "Not really. I can't have people showing up to a murder scene. This isn't the Winchester Mystery House."

He snorted. "You wish you could be the Winchester House."

It didn't take long, but I managed to get in touch with all but one of my guests for the next week. The one who never answered got a long and hopefully coherent message directing her to Toby's bed-and-breakfast. Not that he deserved my referrals, but I'd meant what I said about neighbors helping each other.

Besides, I didn't have time to come up with an alternate solution if I wanted to get this place nice enough to live in before dinner time. That included installing a deadbolt on the cottage door, just in case. Maybe ordering security cameras for the entire property. Cliff could set them up for me when he got back from camping.

Finally, I set my phone down and sighed. "All canceled. Good thing I don't need the money from renting out the rooms."

"The house will be fine. You will be fine. I, however, may perish if you do not get me a scratching post and some catnip. You left all my stuff behind."

That made me feel guilty. In my haste, I hadn't thought to grab anything for my cat, even after he'd helped me get the spell book. Bad Emma. "Sorry, Pink. I figured you could get on without me."

I reached out my hand to scratch behind his ears as an apology. He let me, begrudgingly at first, but after a minute, he settled down beside me and started to purr.

"I'm not leaving you out here alone," he said. "You'll either burn something down or get yourself killed."

With a groan, I grabbed my keys. "Okay, get up. I'll go. Might as well get this over with."

On the way to the car, something caught my attention. I didn't know if it was a movement or a sound or what. But a bang made me turn toward the second guest cabin. The front door wasn't shut all the way. Maybe the police had left it open when they checked over everything? But that didn't explain why the doorknob hung crookedly from the wood.

All the locks had worked perfectly when I'd moved in. I'd checked them the first day while I'd gone around making a list of things I needed to do and ranking them. With all the wildlife from the forest, fixing a door that didn't shout would have been high on the list. Officer Gutierrez hadn't mentioned it, which suggested that the lock had been broken recently.

How recently? Like, within the past hour or so?

"It wasn't like that earlier, right?" I asked my cat. "The door was intact when the police left."

"I think so," he said.

Remembering Pink's comment about ambient magic, I

sent my power into the room, searching for fibers or threads that were warmer than the rest of the room: 98.6 degrees, to be exact.

Instantly, I found it. Warm thread woven into cloth, shaped like a pair of shorts and a shirt. Upright, as in being worn right now.

There was definitely someone hiding in there.

CHAPTER
TEN

"Pink," I whispered, hardly daring to breathe. "Get in the car. I have to call the police. We're getting out of here."

He trotted up to the front door, nosing it open. "The person in there is no danger to me. Or to you."

"How can you know that?"

"I know she's not a danger to me, because she's been giving me treats since last night. Treats that *you* have denied arbitrarily and capriciously."

"All you have to do is apolo—hold on, Pink. There's been a stranger living on my property at the same time *there was a murder* and you didn't think to mention it?"

"Some situations require special handling," he said. "I didn't want you to have to lie to the police."

Why would I lie? The thought was barely half formed when the very obvious answer occurred to me.

"Josie?" I called. "Are you in there? It's okay, everyone is gone."

"Just when I thought you weren't as smart as you look," Pink said softly, disappearing inside.

I waited on the porch. If Josie was hiding in the other guest cottage, she needed to come out and explain herself on her own terms. Going in would just spook her more. If it wasn't Josie, despite Pink's assurances that the person wasn't a danger, I was going to run as fast as my legs would carry me, and I would appreciate the head start.

When the front door swung open all the way, I breathed a sigh of relief. "Where did you go?"

Josie stepped out, looking from side to side hesitantly. "I'm sorry. I panicked."

"Yes, I see that." I tilted my head at her. "Listen, I like you. I'm happy to let you stay if you need a place, and I want to trust you. But you have to trust me, too."

"I'm sorry. I'm used to relying on myself."

"I get it. For years, I was the same way. How about this? You tell me as much of your story as you can, and I'll tell you mine. But before we go any further, I need you to look me in the eye and swear you had nothing to do with what happened to Martha. Because disappearing the way you did looks pretty suspicious."

She met my gaze without hesitation. "I didn't kill her."

Maybe it was naïve of me, but I wanted to believe her. My gut told me Josie's secret had nothing to do with being violent or dangerous. "Why did you run away? Is there anything you need to tell me?"

Josie came further onto the stoop before sitting on the step. I didn't want to move toward her, so I sat on the path. Not the most comfortable, but better than standing. She put her chin in one hand, gazing off into the distance. I was about to give up and head to the store when she finally spoke. "Martha knew my ex-husband. That's what we were arguing about."

"He wasn't very nice to you, was he?" I asked softly. Her

entire demeanor, combined with the bruise on the inside of her wrist, told me the answer.

She shook her head. "I left him. The plan was to move out, get established on my own, and file for divorce once I got some money. That's why I came here—a job that came with a room would allow me to save up that much faster. Even though it's not as far from him as I would have preferred, something told me I'd be okay here. Your grandfather had a reputation for helping people, so I took a leap of faith."

"Makes sense. How did Martha know him?"

"We went to the same church. Ted puts on a big show of being such a great guy, so pious, so wonderful. But—he's not. Not when we're alone."

I'd suspected as much. "I'm sorry."

Tears filled her eyes. She continued as if I hadn't spoken. "Martha told me to go back. She was going to call Ted, tell him she found me here. She insisted it was my wifely duty to take care of my husband, no matter what. I begged her not to. I've been living out of my car for two weeks, moving around because he has friends on the police force. Then I saw your ad."

That explained part of why Martha was so upset to see Josie in the kitchen, but not much. "That's why you ran away when the police arrived. You didn't want anyone to tell Ted you were here."

"I was already packing when you told me she'd been killed. I swear, I didn't have anything to do with it!"

Josie might be desperate, and desperate people did things you wouldn't expect—but I couldn't believe that she had. She could have kept running and been safe. When Martha died, it brought the police here. Josie was worried her husband would hear about the incident. Murder should have been big news in Willow Falls. Now that I thought about it, I was a little surprised no reporters had shown up yet to interview me.

Either way, Josie wouldn't call outside attention to herself.

"I believe you," I said. "And I understand why you wanted to stay hidden from the police. And from the media —they'll probably be here soon."

From the doorway, Pink meowed. "This house is protected. Her husband wouldn't find her here unless someone gave away her location."

"What if someone told him?" I mused.

"Then the protection goes away," Pink said.

Not realizing I wasn't talking to her, Josie said, "If he finds me after I ran out on him, he'll kill me. I can't go back."

My gut told me to trust her, but something Detective Pratt mentioned earlier still bugged me. "I'll let you stay here, on one condition."

"Anything."

"Tell me why you lied about your cooking ability."

She blinked rapidly. "Excuse me?"

"The breakfast you made me was terrible. Detective Pratt told me you're one of the best cooks in the county. He said you win prizes. People fight over the chance to be the first to get your BBQ at the church picnic. What happened? Did you want me to hire Martha?"

"You wouldn't believe me if I told you." She looked away, cheeks flaming.

"Try me," I said.

When she didn't respond, Pink said, "She's a cooking witch."

Josie laughed. "Right. Like that'll work."

"You have cooking magic?" I asked her.

She gasped. "You understood Pink?"

"You understood Pink?" As soon as the words left my mouth, I remembered how he "spoke" with Dottie. She'd said he chose who could understand him. He and Walter chatted all the time. "Maybe we should start over. Hi, I'm Emma. I inherited this mansion from my witch grandfather who also gave me his hearth magic. I live here alone with his ghost and this magical talking cat, who is apparently like seventy years old. Still working that one out."

A wide smile crossed her face. "Hi, Emma. I'm Josie. I have ambient cooking magic, so my emotions get into my food. When I'm happy or excited, everything is delicious. When I'm a little off, it's still pretty good. But when I'm angry, frustrated, or scared—"

Realization dawned. When Martha had called Josie a witch, she wasn't being rude; she was being literal. "Your emotions mess up the spells, and everything tastes like charcoal? Did Martha know?"

"She found out a few weeks ago, during the County Fair. It was so stupid. I just did a minor spell because I didn't have quite enough sugar on hand and she saw me. She accused me of cheating." Josie took a deep breath. "She never liked me. Seeing Martha here when I arrived for the interview left me terrified she would tell you my secret or call my husband or both. All I could think was that he might find me, drag me back home, and that I would be trapped. I was so torn between running and trying to reason with her..."

There was one more thing I needed to know. "Why did you threaten to kill her this morning?"

She blinked at me. "What?"

"When you two were arguing. I was upstairs, in my room. I heard you say, 'I'll kill you!'"

"That wasn't me," Josie said. "Martha told me she'd kill me before letting me give her recipe to Lydia. As if I cared."

My mind raced back to that conversation. Martha's yelling had woken me up. It was the day after I met both women—could I have gotten their voices confused? The commotion traveled up two floors before reaching my ears. "You didn't threaten her at all?"

She shook her head. "I never wanted to cause problems for anyone. All I wanted was a safe place to stay."

Standing, I moved over and put my arms around her. "You never have to go back to that man. I'll make sure of it." Even if I had to find a spell to teleport Ted to Antarctica, he'd never lay a finger on her again.

"I'm sorry I ran away earlier. I got so scared," she said. "Do you have to call the police and tell them I'm here?"

"Not right this second. They can wait," I said. "If you want, I'll go with you to talk to them. As moral support. Or we can bring them back here and go over everything in my cottage.

"I would appreciate that."

"Sorry we can't go back into the main house. The police have banished me for the foreseeable future, so these outbuildings are our homes for now."

"You heard me say I've been living in my car? A dusty cabin is a huge step up."

"It won't be dusty for long," I said. "I was just about to go pick up a few things. Do you need anything? Other than a new doorknob?"

"Sorry about that. I'll pay you back as soon as I can."

"That's not necessary," I said before coming up with a quick lie. "I planned to replace all the locks before using these buildings, anyway. No idea where the original keys are. I haven't been in that cottage at all yet. What else do you need? Sheets, towels? A microwave?"

"No, thanks. I'm okay."

Pink appeared in the open doorway. I hadn't even realized he'd gone inside. "She needs sheets, towels, and some dishes. Also groceries. There's very little in here. Just the bed, an empty bookcase, and a sofa."

Mentally, I added all those things to my shopping list with a nod to the cat. Then Josie's stomach rumbled. After her argument with Martha, the poor woman probably hadn't eaten all day.

"Do you want to come with me?" I asked. "I'm going to be gone awhile. Since we can't use the kitchen, I was going to grab lunch on the way."

She hesitated.

After a minute, I said, "Or I could bring you back a pizza, if you prefer to rest. Things have been stressful. Or can you conjure up food?"

"No, my magic affects existing ingredients. I can't wish food into existence. That would be nice, though." A smile crossed her face. "I like pizza. With extra pepperoni, no peppers."

"Done." I rummaged around in my purse before coming out with a granola bar. "Here. This should tide you over until I get back."

"Thanks, Emma. I promise, you won't regret this."

ELEVEN

Once Pink and I got back from the store with a car packed full of food, linens, and the biggest cat tree that fit in my car, I got to work. With Josie's help, it took a lot less time than expected to clean up both cottages, even with an extended pizza break. She told me more about her relationship with her husband, and I grew increasingly confident in my decision to trust her.

After shopping, cleaning, and dinner, she said she could use some alone time and retired to her cottage for the night. In the morning, I'd encourage her to give a statement to Detective Pratt, but for now, it wasn't worth pushing the issue. If she didn't feel comfortable here, she'd take off again. That was the last thing I wanted.

Still unsettled from the day's events, I went for a walk around the grounds. At the very least, I could poke around and see if anything jumped out at me as a clue. Detective Pratt might be less upset that I didn't call him the second Josie returned if I brought him some evidence. Either way, a stroll outside beat sitting in a tiny room talking to my cat.

Curiosity and lack of a better starting point drew me to the front of the house, where I stood studying the police tape for much too long. Martha's car had been removed from the driveway while I was out—either her son had come to get it or the police towed it.

Josie hadn't parked in front when she'd returned. I'd been too distracted earlier to note that insignificant fact. She must have left her car nearby and walked through the woods. We should talk about that before the police found it and came looking for her.

I walked around the porch, eyes focused on the ground in case anything jumped out at me. The police went over this entire area already, but if I was restless enough to pace around the house, I might as well look for clues that might help me reopen my bed-and-breakfast.

Detective Pratt had mentioned dirt on the floor in the kitchen, which I'd originally figured had been tracked in by me when I returned from the farmers market. But the killer might have gone in the same way. It was completely plausible that they walked up the side stairs and used the kitchen door to sneak up behind Martha. The pink apron I'd found tied around her neck had been hanging right next to the side entrance—now that I thought about it, it was silly not to consider the strong likelihood that the killer had been the one responsible for the dirt inside. Unfortunately, I couldn't see anything on the tile floor through the closed door.

From my vantage point on the front porch, I examined the immediate area. No convenient footprints pointing me at the killer's shoe size, unfortunately. Too many people had been in and out over the past couple of days, including me and Pink. But movement caught my eye.

There, on the porch, something stuck out from between

the steps, fluttering in the slight breeze. Brown, pointy... it basically looked like a normal plant, except I'd cleared this area when I moved in. There shouldn't be any weeds here. Leaning forward, I examined it closer. Just like I thought, it was one of those annoying sticky plants that stuck brambles into you and you didn't notice until you were a quarter mile away and had a stupid brown vine trailing behind you and holes in your socks.

So I'd heard.

Anyway, the important thing was, when I'd first moved here, I'd gone a bit overboard with the Round Up, and we shouldn't have any of these things within two hundred feet of the house. I carefully skirted them now, and Pink was too smart to get caught in brambles. But it might have gotten caught on the killer's clothes and been dragged. I didn't want to touch it in case it was a clue, but I zoomed in and took a picture with my phone.

"Where did you come from?" I murmured, looking at the image.

This property covered a couple of acres, many of them wooded. There were a lot of places for someone to hide. I didn't have any idea how many access points there were, but lots of the trails behind the property were open to the public. Anyone could have parked, hiked over, and then walked in. But who knew Martha was here? She'd only started the job this morning.

It felt like a thousand hours ago.

Pink had said that this property was shielded from people who didn't know about it. Granted, Walter lived in the town his whole life, so most of the locals were probably aware of the house's existence. But for someone to specifically come here to kill Martha, they had to be aware I'd hired her, right? There was no other reason for her to be here.

Who knew? Her family, most likely. Any friends. The people she'd spoken with at the farmers market. Possibly anyone else who had been there this morning when Martha arrived.

And anyone they told about the fight.

Basically, the entire town. News spread fast around here.

Directly off the kitchen steps lay the garden, overgrown to where I avoided these stairs while using the porch. I'd had no time to look at it, and my gardening skills were about on par with my baking abilities. Definitely something to leave to the professionals. To my knowledge, there were no wild brambles growing in there.

I studied the stone paths, but I didn't even know what to look for. Some plants looked a bit mushed, but there were so many of them I could barely see the dirt beneath. Anyone could have walked through without leaving foot-prints. In fact, because this was the way to Toby's house, most likely, he and Cliff had both walked through in the past twenty-four hours. As much as Toby hated me, I didn't think he had any reason to dislike Martha. Cliff was off camping, so I couldn't ask if he'd come through the garden earlier. The plants also could have been stepped on by a police officer looking for clues.

Moving on, I headed to the large barn off the side of the house. Since the large double doors weren't usable, I bypassed them and went to the smaller, human-sized side door. It swung open, and I peeked inside the space, still not knowing what I hoped to find.

At some point, Walter had converted the building to a garage, if the ancient car inside was any sign. Or maybe long-term storage. There was so much dust covering the vehicle, I could hardly tell what color it was supposed to be, unless hideous brown was big forty years ago. The car didn't appear to have been drivable within my lifetime. I assumed it belonged to me, but did I really want to restore a 1981 Pontiac Bonneville? The bike parked by the far wall seemed like a more reliable form of transportation if needed.

A mess of footprints inside the door straightened out and led to a ladder, which leaned up against the loft. I spotted at least a couple of different sizes. My guess was they belonged to one or more police officers. Or possibly Josie, before she'd broken into the cottage. I'd have to ask her about it later.

The ladder itself was missing a couple of rungs, which was one of many reasons I'd never tried to climb it. But before venturing any further into the building, I needed to be one hundred percent sure I was alone. The only way to do that was to explore. Pulling out a thread of magic, I fed it into the loft, leading it to expand, search out any other cloth.

Against the far wall of the loft, found a large rectangle which, if I was reading things correctly, had several holes. The fabric seemed to be folded over on itself several times. It felt like an old blanket, and had probably been there for decades.

A few feet to the left, I sensed something else that made me stop. Cloth, probably cotton. Three or four feet long with sleeves and finished edges. Definitely clothing.

My heart pounded.

"Hello?" I called. "Josie, is that you?"

No answer.

My friend would reply if she were there, but she also

couldn't have left her cottage and gotten here so quickly. Maybe I should leave and call the police. But how to tell them I'd magically uncovered clothing in the loft? Besides, when I'd sensed Josie earlier, her body heat was the thing that alerted me. Whatever lurked up there, it was the same temperature as the rest of the room—about sixty-five degrees.

If there was a living person up there, they'd need my help.

With a deep breath, I said a prayer that the ladder would hold my weight before beginning my climb. One rung at a time, I pulled myself upward, praying that I didn't tumble to the ground. If my magic could save me, I didn't know how yet.

What felt like an hour later, I poked my head over the bottom of the loft and peeked inside. "Anyone there?"

Still no reply. It was too dark to see without my flashlight, and I didn't feel all that confident holding the ladder with one hand while shining a light around with the other.

This was ridiculous. Who did I think I was, Jessica Fletcher? I should go down to the ground, get out of here, and call the police.

But at this range, the cloth I'd found seemed even less threatening. Nothing moved in the loft area. I cocked my head to listen, but there wasn't a sound. After pulling myself up to the top, I dusted my hands and grabbed my phone. A couple of quick taps and a beam shone around the mostly empty space. Raising it, I pointed the light at the fabric I'd sensed.

When the human form came into view, I stiffened. A scream rose in my throat. Then I realized that it still hadn't moved. It also had no head.

"Hello?"

Nothing.

Cautiously, I took a small step forward.

A dress form sat in front of me.

I'd been afraid of what appeared to be an old flapper costume. It was super cute—short and bright red, with fringe. A matching boa draped around the top.

Nothing else.

Now I felt silly, being afraid of a costume.

At least the item in the corner turned out to be, as expected, a moth-eaten blanket. I left it there, then turned to debate how to get the dress form down to the ground. It could be useful once cleaned.

Since I didn't have a death wish, trying to carry it down the ladder wasn't an option. I'd have to come back with some rope to lower it. For now, I needed to keep searching for clues, and there weren't any up here.

A stroll around the entire building showed more dirt, signs of mice, and nothing to suggest who killed Martha. After leaving the barn, I decided to wander the grounds. My magic went out ahead, looking for any people who weren't supposed to be here.

As the sun set, a chill filled the air. With each step, I became more and more aware that someone had been killed on this very property by an unknown person. While there was no reason to think the murderer would have stuck around, but it made sense to be on the alert.

The property covered about four acres, which would take me quite a while to walk on a day when I wasn't emotionally and physically exhausted. Since I wasn't about to enter the woods this late in the day, I stayed about a foot inside the tree line. This path could be done in less than an hour on a good day.

No people. Lots of birds. It was peaceful.

On the way back, I crossed behind the pool house. The police tape blocking off the front door was nowhere to be seen back here. The officers hadn't told me what they'd found, but I had no intention of going inside.

Something made me pause. The scene didn't look quite right. Since getting the lawn cleaned up hadn't been a priority, high grass covered this area as far as the eye could see. Except the spot directly under the back window of the pool house.

I moved closer. It was subtle, but something had flattened the grass in this spot. Not all of it bounced back. No footprints in the dirt, but definitely had someone been through here. With my power, I searched the room. It appeared to be empty of humans, although my magic found lots of rectangular objects that felt like beach towels.

The window was closed. There was no way to tell if was locked without trying to open it, and leaving fingerprints at the scene of a crime seemed like a bad idea. Still, I would have bet my fortune that a person had been in here within the past couple of days.

Turning around, I looked for a stick or something I could use to check the window without touching it. The rays from the setting sun shifted straight into my eyes, making it impossible to see anything.

No, wait. The sun should be behind me. Squinting, I turned to examine the ground. Rays of light were bouncing off something lying in the flattened area of the grass. With the sun blinding me, I couldn't tell what it was. My powers told me that it wasn't thread, but roughly six billion things in existence were not thread. It might be the pull tab from a soda can, thrown away years ago.

Nope.

When I squatted down, the tree line blocked the sun's

rays and let me see once again. Two golden rings lying in the dirt. One a plain gold circle, the other topped with a small diamond. I'd seen both of those rings before, on Martha. She wore them to the interview: her wedding rings.

What were they doing here?

TWELVE

When Detective Pratt questioned me earlier, he'd said they didn't think Martha's death was part of a burglary because her purse hadn't been taken. But apparently, the murderer had stripped her wedding rings from her fingers—why? Were they trying to make it look like a theft but didn't see her purse in the pantry? Did someone kill Martha to steal the rings and then decide they didn't want them? Had the murderer just accidentally dropped the rings in a bit of random good luck? None of that made sense.

I couldn't answer any of those questions, but it was long past time to call the police and let them know what I'd found. Hopefully Detective Pratt had gone home and gotten some sleep after leaving this morning.

Although I'd promised Josie not to call the police until she was ready, I couldn't ignore this evidence. I didn't want to touch anything, and I couldn't risk the possibility that the killer would realize the rings were gone and come back to find them. All I could do was hope Detective Pratt could fingerprint such small items. Maybe that would help them find the killer.

Before pulling out my phone, I knocked on Josie's door to explain what had happened. "If you don't want to stick around, I understand. But at some point, you have to face them. Maybe it's better to do it now."

She swallowed hard before nodding. "Let's do it."

Detective Pratt sounded tired when he answered, but he perked up considerably when I told him I'd found both Josie and some clues. "You didn't touch anything, did you?"

"Of course not! I've seen *Law & Order*. My goal is to get back inside my house, not to get arrested for tampering with the evidence."

"Sorry. I just have to be sure. Where is Mrs. Ross now?"

"I'm letting her stay in one of the other guest cottages."

"Can you see if she leaves?"

"Only if I plaster my nose against the windows." I debated whether to tell him why she'd run away. It wasn't my secret, but at the end of the day, if the police went looking for her at the home where her husband lived, it could go back. "She came here to hide from her husband. Please don't let him know she's here. I'm positive she can't go home, but because she's not hiding from the police. Josie didn't kill Martha. I'd stake my life on it."

"You might be doing just that, letting her stay."

When Detective Pratt arrived, I took him around the side of the house and pointed at the porch steps. "I found these dead plants outside the kitchen entrance. I swear they weren't there earlier. Do you think the killer could have brought them in?"

"Yeah, maybe." He shone a flashlight at the steps, since we were losing the light fast. "Oh, those. Brambles. Those are everywhere."

My face fell. "Does that mean you won't be able to figure out how they got to my porch?"

"When I was a child, I played in these woods all the time. Did you know your grandfather used to host an Easter Egg Hunt? It was a great time. The only problem was, if you took a wrong step, you'd find these brambles wrapped halfway up your leg. Exactly like these."

With that, I deflated. "So when you say everywhere, you mean it."

"Anyone who walked to the farmers market could have picked them up. Or a neighbor's house, or even if someone just went for a walk through the trees."

I sighed. "Well, it was worth asking."

"There aren't any on your driveway, though."

"You mean, if I found this plant on the kitchen porch, it probably didn't come from someone who parked in the driveway and walked up to the kitchen?"

"Exactly."

Detective Pratt was more interested in the flattened grass beneath the pool house window. "Is this usually locked?"

"I have no idea," I said. "I've only been out here once."

He looked from the ground to the window and back, then nodded. "Good eye. I wouldn't be surprised if the killer came through here. I'll get a team out here to dust for prints in the morning. Meanwhile, stay away from this area."

The thought of a killer hiding in my pool house even as I stumbled across Martha's body made me shiver. "No problem. I may never leave my cottage again."

"That's not necessary." He gave me a half-smile, then squatted down beside the rings. "Are you sure these belonged to the victim?"

"Not one hundred percent, but they're similar to the

ones she wore yesterday morning. I only caught a brief glimpse. Why? Does Martha still have her rings?"

He shook his head. "That was one detail we didn't tell anyone. Before we took her away, we noticed an indentation on her ring finger. We wanted to follow-up with the family to be sure. Martha's husband died years ago; she might have taken off her rings."

"But she didn't," I said, remembering how Martha looked at her husband when that door opened. "She loved him until the day she died."

Detective Pratt shot me a curious look. "I thought you said you didn't know her well."

"She let a few things slip." Maybe it was good that she'd gone into the light so quickly—if she were here sharing more things I wasn't supposed to know, I could find myself moved to the top of the suspect list.

He dropped a marker on the ground and spoke into his radio, calling someone to come pick up the rings. Then he asked me to take him to Josie.

We found her inside her cottage, sitting at the kitchen table.

Detective Pratt turned to me. "Are you a lawyer?"

"No, why?"

He pointed at the door. "Out."

When I hesitated, he crossed his arms. "We could do this at the police station instead."

Yikes. Not what I wanted at all.

Josie said, "It's fine. I'll be okay."

She looked terrified, but since refusing to leave would only make matters worse, I went to wait out on the porch. The door slammed in my face. Then it bounced open because I hadn't replaced the lock yet. Something scraped across the floor—he must be dragging a chair from the table. Sure enough, the door closed a second time and this time it stayed shut.

As quietly as I could, I slunk around to find an open window. Pink appeared at my feet. "Did it ever occur to you that you're violating Josie's privacy?"

"I'm trying to stop her from getting arrested," I hissed.

"Sitting here isn't going to clear her name. If you want to help, talk her into filing charges against her husband. Hire her a lawyer. Help her find her confidence. Better yet, find the real killer."

He was right. Nothing Josie told Detective Pratt would help me figure out who killed Martha. If she had seen or heard anything, she would have told me. Frustrated, I settled onto the porch steps to wait for the detective to leave.

By the time the interview ended, I'd nearly dozed off with my head against the porch railing. I jumped at the sound of the chair scraping across the floor, away from me. That gave me about twenty seconds to stand up and act like I hadn't been waiting for them to come out.

"Can I help you with something?" Detective Pratt asked.

My mind went completely blank under his scrutiny. I couldn't even have told him my name. Finally, I shook my head. "No. How's Josie?"

"She's all yours," he said. "But before I go, there's one more thing."

"Yeah?"

"I know you're frustrated to have your business put on hold so soon after opening. But I don't want you scrounging around looking for evidence. Leave that to the profession-als. You can reopen once it's safe."

The professionals had actually been here and missed

the evidence that I'd found, but pointing that out didn't seem likely to help my cause. "I was just out for a walk."

"Sure you were." He moved down the path, then turned back as I headed for the door. "I know what you're doing. No more amateur sleuthing. No talking to potential suspects. This is a matter for the police. If I catch you going inside that house before it's cleared, I'll have you arrested for interfering with an investigation. Are we clear?"

I gulped. "Yes, sir."

CHAPTER
THIRTEEN

The next morning, I awoke to bright sunlight streaming through the window and someone calling my name. For a minute, I thought it was Josie—but it would make more sense for her to simply knock on my door. Besides, it was a male voice. Detective Pratt would most likely call rather than dropping by unannounced. And it didn't sound like Walter, who I'd yet to see outside of the mansion. Could he roam the entire property or just the house?

Someone else was here.

What time was it? The bright sunlight suggested daytime, but we lived in the northern part of the state and it was August. Sunlight began early.

"Emma? Are you okay?"

Hold on. I knew that voice. Was I expecting someone? I didn't think so, but I'd only been awake about twelve seconds and it usually took me a little longer to get it together in the mornings. Caffeine was needed before the brain started to function.

I was reaching for my phone on the nightstand beside

the bed when the stranger came closer and called for me again. This time his voice sounded familiar. Cliff! With everything that happened, I'd completely forgotten he was supposed to start work on the bathroom this morning.

Tossing on a robe purchased the day before, I hurried to the front door of the cottage and flung it open. "Over here! Sorry!"

He jogged up, relief crossing his features when he saw me. "There you are! I saw the police tape and thought something happened to you. You didn't answer your phone."

"I turned it off when I went to bed," I said. "Guess I'll have to quit that once the B&B is up and running. Then again, I should be back to sleeping upstairs in my room by then."

"Why are you out here? What's going on?"

In such a small town, it surprised me he wouldn't already know. "You didn't hear? My new chef—Martha Armstrong—was murdered."

"Oh, no! That's terrible. Here?"

I nodded.

"When?"

"Yesterday morning. Your dad didn't mention it?"

"I haven't seen him," Cliff said. "After I left here, I went to the hardware store to pick up some tile samples for you, and then I headed up north. Went fishing and set up camp, then stayed until this morning. Dad was still asleep when I got home. I came to see you after dropping off my gear. Now I'm glad I did. That must have been terrible."

His kind words made me smile. "I'm sorry I forgot you were coming. Let me get dressed, and we'll talk. Unfortunately, as the police tape may have indicated, I can't let you inside the house. But there's a coffeemaker here in the cottage."

"I've got a better idea. Let's take a walk down to the farmers market and get a real breakfast. If you haven't tried the burrito stand yet, you're in for a treat. On the way, you can tell me what happened."

"Burritos for breakfast?"

"Trust me. Best bacon and eggs you've ever had."

That sounded amazing. It only took me five minutes to run a brush through my hair, pull on a pair of shorts and a tank top in preparation for the heat, and... no. I didn't need any make-up. This wasn't a date. We were going to talk about bathroom fixtures. Cliff wasn't interested in me, and I didn't have the time or energy to be interested in him.

Even if he was cute. And considerate.

My stomach growled, putting an end to the internal debate. Makeup would take longer and therefore delay my breakfast. I pinched my cheeks, grabbed my vanilla-flavored lip moisturizer, and slid my phone and wallet into my pockets.

As we walked down the forest path, Cliff listened while I talked about the shock of finding Martha, the distress at realizing someone had come into my house and killed her, and the frustration of having to move into the cottage until the police finished their investigation. I kept my eyes peeled for brambles until I spotted the tenth or so patch. Detective Pratt was right: everywhere. My "clue" was a dead end.

"Are you okay?" Cliff asked. "If you're scared being alone, you can stay at our place. I'm not being forward—we've got lots of rooms."

I smiled at him. "Thanks, but I'm okay. The police didn't seem to think there was any reason for the killer to come back."

"Well, if you need anything, day or night, call me. The path is about half a mile. I can run it in five minutes flat." I raised an eyebrow at him, and he laughed. "Well, I could as a kid. My older brother and I used to race. It was a constant battle to see who was better. He had the advantage, being older, but I've got longer legs."

"So you beat him every time?"

"Nah. Half the time, he'd trip me. Older brothers cheat."

We arrived at the farmers market as the morning rush was dwindling. Lots of people sat at the picnic tables, most of them appearing to be nearly done with their meals. The scent of freshly brewed coffee filled the air, along with the unmistakable mixture of cinnamon, butter, and sugar that signaled the best thing in the world: breakfast pastries.

I was halfway to Beth's stall for some still-warm muffins when Cliff pulled me back. "Not so fast. I know that smells good, but trust me. You've got to try the burritos."

Did I? Part of me wanted to go for the pastries just because I hated some guy telling me what I wanted to eat. But he invited me to try the burritos, and protein would help me get through what promised to be a very long morning. Then I caught sight of the workers bustling around the stall. Massive tortillas being flamed-grilled on the stove, scrambled eggs, bacon...Whatever I'd expected, this wasn't it.

"If that tastes half as good as it looks, I'm never eating anything else for the rest of my life," I said.

"Prepare to have your taste buds dazzled." He grinned at me, which made my whole body more alert.

I couldn't decide between the chorizo-and-salsa-filled burrito or the maple-bacon one, so we ordered both and split them. When the cook handed me the bag, I clutched it to my chest, only half-joking about not sharing. Cliff took our coffees and led me to a vacant spot at a nearby picnic table so we could dig in.

Oh, wow. The first bite was heaven. The spicy sausage and the tangy salsa danced on my tongue and the whole thing was so amazing, I almost forgot to chew. Unbelievably, when I switched to the maple bacon for my second bite, it was equally good. I couldn't even pick a favorite. Better to keep taste-testing. Yes, that one was amazing. So was this one. And the first one.

We were quiet for several long, delicious minutes other than chewing and my yummy sounds.

"Was I right?" Cliff asked.

"I will never doubt you again," I said.

Once I'd taken the edge off my hunger, I remembered what he told me on the way here. "You and your brother used to race back and forth between the properties, huh? Does that mean you knew my grandfather?"

"Walter? Yeah, sure. Everyone knew Old Walt." He wiped his mouth before continuing. "It's a shame you never got to meet him. He was a good guy."

"Was Walter friends with your father?"

"He was friends with everyone. The life of every party."

That tracked with what I knew about him, especially the Easter Egg Hunt Detective Pratt mentioned. Slowly, a picture of the man behind the ghost was emerging. Everybody had loved him. He'd always been surrounded by people. The loneliness of death must have come as quite a shock. Poor guy. All this time, he'd been hanging around on this plane, unable to interact with anyone. Good thing I moved in instead of some stranger who wouldn't see him.

"Did he seem lonely?" I asked. "His lawyer said he never married."

"If he was, I never saw it. He seemed like a happy guy,

but I was a teenager when he died." Cliff paused, like a memory hit him, and then chuckled. "Once, I asked him why he lived all by himself in such a big house. Dad was mortified."

"I bet! What did he say?"

"Told me he snored so loud, the house shook. No one was willing to live with him."

That fit with the ghost I knew so well, I burst into laughter. People turned to look, which made me want to hide under the table. "I guess I shouldn't be having such a good time after someone died in my house."

Reaching across the table, Cliff took my hand. "Listen. You didn't want Martha dead. You're not happy she's gone, are you?"

"Definitely not. I feel terrible."

"Then there's no reason to feel guilty about enjoying yourself. You're not responsible for everything that happens on your property. If you're going to run a bed-and-breakfast, you'll want to keep that in mind. It's impossible to control everyone who walks through those doors. Trying will make you miserable."

I gave him a small smile. "Thanks. I just wish I knew who did it. I'd like to move back in and get things running as soon as possible."

"That's a job for the police, not the hotel operator. The one thing we know about the person who killed Martha is that they can be dangerous. I don't want you to get hurt."

"Don't worry. I'm not going to get too close. I just want Martha put to rest so I can move forward. This place was supposed to be a new life for me, a way of starting over. I hate that it's been shut down before it could get off the ground. I feel like a butterfly interrupted in the middle of chrysalis."

"That's understandable. Everything will come together, Emma. Just give it time. Focus on what you can control."

Good idea. What could I control? Working on my magic? Maybe. Gaining information? At least I was in the right place for that. When I'd been here on Tuesday morning, the woman who sold me the pastries told me Martha had an argument with her sister. Were they here now?

Shading my eyes, I peered into the stand. There was Beth, working the counter and chatting with customers. Someone moved around in the back. It might be her sister, Lydia. Only one way to find out. I stood up.

"Ready to head back?"

"Not yet," I said. "I want to get something to snack on later. Stay here and finish your coffee."

When I approached the stand, I studied Lydia. She was taller than me, muscular in the way that bakers often are. Kneading dough must make for powerful arms—Martha had them, too. Too bad they hadn't helped her save herself.

Flour dusted Lydia's hairnet-covered blond hair and streaked her cheeks. She and Martha apparently had a lot in common. When she spotted me watching, she came over. "Hello. Can I help you?"

"I'm Emma Faden," I said. "I operate a bed-and-breakfast down the trail a bit. I'm hoping we can work out an arrangement for daily pastries until I get a chef installed to serve a hot breakfast."

Since Josie was still terrified of her ex and stressed by the murder investigation, I'd rather not take a chance on her baking for third parties until we got a better handle on her emotions. At the moment, I had only Detective Pratt's word that she could cook at all.

Lydia held up her hands to avoid shaking mine. Both were covered in plastic gloves, and a white bandage wrapped her left palm. "I'm just the baker. For business stuff, talk to Beth."

Since Beth was still chatting with their customers, I ignored the hint. "I had one of your muffins the other day. It was delicious."

She beamed. "Thank you! They've won awards, you know."

"Congratulations! You don't sell cookbooks, do you? I'd love the recipe."

"You know, I don't, but I've been thinking about it. I wanted a few of the local women to put together a book with all our fair-winning creations over the years. It should do well, since people like our stuff so much." She sighed and shook her head. "It's not going to happen, though."

"Why won't it happen?"

"Our local prize-winning cinnamon rolls. The woman who made them refuses to participate. Refused, I mean. She passed away." Lydia sniffled and swiped at one eye with a towel. "You knew Martha, right?"

"We'd only just met. Were you close?"

She barked out a laugh. "Hardly. Long-time acquaintances, though."

"Still, I'm sorry for your loss."

"Thank you." She pointed toward the end of the counter. "Sister's free. I've got work to do."

Moving toward the register, I thought about our conversation. Lydia didn't mention arguing with Martha the morning she died. She wasn't here when I dropped by the farmers market, around the same time Martha got killed. She could have been anywhere.

With those muscular forearms, Lydia certainly had the strength to strangle someone. She might have thought it appropriate to use an apron. Plus, her hands were bandaged. From something innocent, or had Martha scratched Lydia while fighting for her life?

Although I didn't particularly need to talk to Beth, it might look suspicious if I just walked away. Quickly I repeated my lie about supplying baked goods to the bed-and-breakfast and got her card. If she followed up, I'd say I changed my mind because her sister killed my first cook.

Or, you know, some other reason.

After that, Cliff and I decided to head back. Our walk back through the woods didn't have the same vibe as the way to the farmers market. Maybe I was too distracted, but I couldn't think of much to say. When we reached the place where the trail parted, one side going toward my home and the other to his, Cliff hesitated. I thanked him for breakfast, promised to call him as soon as he could start work on the bathroom, and headed home. He looked a bit disappointed, which left me torn. Part of me wanted to explore this thing, see if we could be something more than contractor and customer. But the timing was awful. It was impossible to think about getting involved with someone with Martha's death overshadowing everything.

One thing I knew for sure. I needed answers.

FOURTEEN

Back at the mansion, Josie was weeding the garden outside the kitchen door. My eyes pointlessly searched the ground for brambles. I couldn't help myself. "Hey. I brought you breakfast."

She sat back on her heels and took a bite. "You are a darling. Thank you."

"My pleasure. Especially since, apparently, you're gardening for me?" She hadn't mentioned any knowledge of or talent for gardening, but she couldn't possibly make the place look worse.

"Keeping my hands busy helps clear my head."

"You didn't think of anything interesting, did you?"

"You mean like, a clue to tell me who killed Martha?"

My cheeks grew warm. I hadn't meant to be that obvious. Avoiding her gaze, I said, "Maybe if we could give the police a push in the right direction, we might be allowed to move back inside soon."

"I understand. Unfortunately, unless it was an over-grown tomato bush that did the deed, I'm not sure I can help. But I'll let you know if anything seems out of the ordinary. Besides all these weeds."

"Thanks." I held up my bag. "Do you want another one for while you work?"

She shook her head as she chewed another bite. "No, this should be fine. But I might swing by for another one later."

"I'll leave it on your doorstep," I said. With what I had planned, it was better she didn't come looking for me.

From the look of things, Josie would be occupied for ages. That gave me plenty of time to talk to Walter if I could get inside the mansion. Maybe he'd remember something useful if we talked about yesterday morning. Or he could help me come up with a spell. Things that would be better to do while my guest wasn't around to ask questions. Josie knew about my magic and my cat, but we hadn't talked about the ghost. Walter might not want too many people to know about him.

Then again, based on what I'd heard, he might want me to throw him a party to announce his triumphant return as reigning spector. Something for Future Emma to contemplate.

After pausing at Josie's place to drop off more pastries, I made a beeline for the book hidden under the mattress in my cottage. Not the most ingenious of hiding places, but the book itself was covered in protection spells. This piece belonged to Walter, and it had been guarded so only his rightful heir could open it. Once I'd learned the basics, I'd repeated the spells, placing an additional layer over the magic laid by my grandfather so many years ago. No reason to take chances: I wasn't sure how long my grandfather's spells would last after his death.

The grimoire was old and heavy, its worn pages turning

yellow. Only the magic in the book kept the paper from crumbling. Hidden under it was my own, much-newer spell book I'd started a few weeks ago in a purple Lisa Frank notebook depicting unicorns playing on a rainbow. I liked that it reminded me of my childhood. Pink called it gaudy.

I'd refused to give him treats until he apologized. Which should happen any day now.

Not sure what I was looking for, I flipped through the pages of the older tome. Did Walter have a truth spell? Something to make people confess? That would only help if Lydia was the killer, unless I wanted to try it on everyone I met.

Nothing said, "Come to my bed-and-breakfast, I'm normal" like walking around town asking every single person if they'd killed someone while chanting under your breath. It might be useful once I'd narrowed the list, but not now.

Mostly, it looked like Walter's powers were the same as mine. He also had hearth powers, and that lent itself to general cleaning magic. He had a spell for growing tomatoes. One for clothes to wash and fold themselves. Now that I would memorize.

Pink bounded into the room and hopped onto my mattress before plopping down on the corner nearest me. "That's not going to help."

"Shouldn't my protection spells keep you out?"

"The spells are for people, not cats."

"Maybe I can find a cat spell," I grumbled at him, but I was actually happy to have him at my side. "What do you mean, the book won't help?"

"Truth spells are tricky. An experienced witch could conjure up a truth potion if you had the right recipe, but that requires getting the subject to consume it. That's impossible until you have a likely suspect."

"Lydia is my likely suspect, but I don't see her drinking anything I give her." I sighed, flopped back onto my pillows. "Okay, then, how do I find out what happened?"

"Why do you care? Let the police do their jobs. Focus on your magic and scratching behind my ears."

"I promised Josie I would help," I said, although I did reach over to do as he asked. "She had motive and opportunity. She's terrified the police will arrest her and it'll make the news and her ex-husband will find her. I can't let that happen if there's any way to avoid it."

Pink studied me for so long, I started to wonder if he'd fallen asleep with his eyes open. "Talk to Walter. Maybe he knows a spell that isn't in the book."

"Do you think he'll help? He made it seem like he didn't want to get involved."

"What he wants," Pink said, "is a relationship with his granddaughter. Only you can give him that."

"Most relationships take time to establish."

"That may be true, but you've got history on your side. Also, you look exactly like your grandmother."

I perked up at his words. "You think so? We didn't have any pictures of Grandma when she was young—only after her hair had gone gray. People said we had the same eyes, though."

"Same hazel eyes, same long red hair, same big heart," Pink said. "There should be pictures. Walter had one by his bedside until the day he died."

"That's both very touching and very sad."

"He loved her, even after she left him."

"Why did she leave?"

"That's not for me to tell you," he said. "Ask him."

He had a point. However, I still didn't know how to get into the house without getting in trouble with Detective Pratt. Unless I could teleport or fly up to the chimney, I needed a way to summon a ghost to me. Back to the spell book. I paged through it, looking for anything that might be useful.

The majority of the pages were blank. How did I make the book give up its secrets?

Putting on my most beseeching expression, I said, "Please show me a spell that will let me into my house without getting arrested."

Nothing happened.

"Pretty please?"

Pink said, "The book isn't sentient."

"Then how does it know when I'm ready for a given spell?"

"It doesn't. You also can't convince the book to share anything before you're ready to learn it. Walter's spells were set up to help you find your way in steps since he didn't know if he'd be able to teach you himself."

"That's so annoying. Maybe it made sense when he died —I was only sixteen. But now? I'm not a child. I know how to pace myself."

"Says the woman who tried to rebuild the whole house before unlocking the front door on the day she arrived."

Hmmph. Everyone said they wanted a magic cat, but then the cat started talking...

"Are you here to help?" I asked grumpily.

Maybe the answer was in my ambient magic. There had to be some way to use the world around me to figure out what had happened. If the apron were here, I could ask it to show me Martha's death. Unfortunately, Detective Pratt wasn't likely to give it to me.

What about Lydia? Could I do a spell on the clothes she had worn on Tuesday, ask them to show me everywhere she went?

Sure. I'd just go back to the farmers market and ask her nicely to let me raid her dirty laundry so I could accuse her of murder.

I could figure this out. I had to figure this out. After giving Pink one more scratch behind the ears, I sat up and took the book into my lap again.

When I was in high school, I'd studied Wicca. The whole religion fascinated me. But at the time, every spell I attempted failed. Eventually I'd drifted away. Let myself believe that it wasn't for me. Now that I knew I'd been cursed, it explained both why I'd been drawn to witchcraft initially and why my spells never worked.

Now, my hearth spells went well. Every page in this book that taught me about the home, keeping house, etc. worked like a dream. But I still needed a spell to cast in order to perform magic, and nothing in front of me was useful.

A groan escaped me. Pink curled up beside me, purring. I stroked his silky fur to clear my head. I wish I could say something brilliant popped into my brain as a result, but at least some of the frustration dissipated.

"This is so annoying," I grumbled. "Walter can't teach me anything if we're in different houses. Can't I just, I don't know, reach for his ghostly clothes and pull them toward me?"

"That might work if his clothes were real," Pink said. "You have a strong ability to manipulate thread, which includes cloth. But in this case, no. Why don't you use the tunnel?"

CHAPTER

FIFTEEN

At Pink's blasé suggestion, I gaped at him like it was my first time hearing a talking cat. "Tunnel? *There's a tunnel?* To the big house?"

"Oh, yes. These cottages were built as servants' quarters. In the winter, the servants didn't have twenty minutes to wade through the snow and ice between here and the main house. Plus, you didn't want them tracking in slush when they got there. The tunnels were part of the original plans."

"Is that something else you didn't think I was ready to know?" I tried not to let my aggravation seep into every word, but okay, I didn't try very hard.

He shook his head. "I forgot. While there were rumors of Walter's father using them to visit his mistress without his wife realizing it, no one has mentioned the tunnels in ages. The only person who lived here toward the end of Walter's life was his housekeeper and cook. Her rooms were on the second floor. They didn't have cell phones—she needed to hear him call her."

"Okay, fine. I forgive you for not telling me. Now let's go."

When we'd been in the basement yesterday, I hadn't spent a lot of time examining the space, but I'd only been looking for cleaning supplies. Now, I stood in the middle of the room, hands on my hips, peering at the walls. The solid walls, with no cracks or openings.

"Is this some kind of joke?" I asked, pushing at the solid surface on the side facing the mansion. It didn't budge.

"You didn't think just anyone could find the tunnels, did you?" Pink asked. "Reach for them. Use your magic."

"I can't!" It took everything in me to resist stomping my foot like a petulant child. This was so frustrating. "I'll get in trouble with the stupid witch police."

Pink sat back and stared at me for a long minute before he casually began to lick one paw. "Actually, you won't."

"What? You heard Dottie—"

"She was just trying to scare you."

"Excuse me?"

"The OME can't tell when a person uses magic. If they could, they'd be inundated with reports all day long. She knew you'd changed the house because she heard the blast and smelled the smoke. She was about a block behind us when we pulled up."

I gaped at him. "Are you serious right now?"

"Very much so. Don't get me wrong. There are rules, and there are serious consequences for violating the bigger ones. You can't use magic to kill someone, for example, or bring someone back to life."

I shuddered at the thought. "But I can use my magic for normal things without getting in trouble?"

"Yes, absolutely. That's what she and I were talking about before she left. I told her it wasn't wise to put a leash on you. She insisted you would be safer this way. I promised not to say anything unless necessary."

"Well, thanks for deeming it necessary now, I guess."

"You're welcome. I want to go back to the mansion as badly as you do, and apparently, unless I help you solve this mystery, it's not going to happen soon. My treats are still in there."

When he put it that way, my fading exasperation returned. "So where's the tunnel?"

He pointed at the wall nearest the house and told me the spell. Closing my eyes, I took a deep breath, pointed with both hands, and repeated the incantation.

A grinding sound filled the air. A rush of wind blew past my face.

When I opened my eyes, a piece of the wall had shifted aside to reveal a dark opening. Using my phone's flashlight, I went inside. The ground was smooth, and the air was cool. It looked pretty well maintained for something no one had entered in decades. The beauty of magical maintanence.

Less than a minute later, I repeated the spell to open the door that took me into the basement of the mansion. The room on the other side was pitch black. I could only see a few inches beyond the doorway, even with my flashlight app.

"Do you want to go first?" I asked my cat. "I don't know what's in there."

"Humans," he grumbled with a shake of his head. "Afraid of a little darkness. Fine, let the cat check it out."

"I appreciate you," I said.

"Not enough." He bounded into the opening, only to return a moment later. "Nothing to see. There's a light switch at the bottom of the stairs."

The bulb over the staircase did little to illuminate the space. Lots of dark corners. A bit of dust. Some cobwebs. Nothing else.

I did a quick spell to bring more light into the room, making a note to replace the bulb with something brighter. Even if I didn't come down here often, I needed to see when I did.

Still nothing to see, although Pink raced past me to attack the bottom stair.

"Thanks for nothing," I said. "What am I doing here?"

"You're looking for ways to connect with your grandfather."

"He isn't here," I pointed out. "Neither is any of his stuff. Where are the boxes? I should have inherited anything that wasn't sold by the estate. Where did he keep his memories?"

Walter shimmered into view in front of me. "They're spelled. You think I want just anyone going through my stuff?"

"I'm not just anyone," I pointed out. "I'm your grand-daughter. Vera's granddaughter. I'd hoped to find pictures of her."

"Hmmph."

"You know, Grandma always said I got my stubborn-ness from her side of the family, but I'm thinking she may not have been one hundred percent truthful about that."

A smile crossed his lips. "She was set in her ways, wasn't she?"

"She would do anything to avoid being wrong. One time, she was making a casserole for dinner, but she misread the recipe. Only used a quarter cup of water for the rice. Oh, but she swore up and down that she could see perfectly, that she'd done it all right, and that the rice was *supposed* to be crunchy."

He chuckled. "That sounds like Vera."

"You really miss her, don't you?"

"Every day. Both during my life and beyond."

"Me, too," I said. "I'm sorry you've been trapped here all this time."

"Funny you should mention that," he said. "I've been thinking about ways you can help me."

"I can untrap you? How?"

"You're a witch. Do a spell."

That gave me pause. "Really? There's a spell for that? To make you alive? Or give you a form or something?"

He shook his head. "No, no. But you could create a magical object, one that would allow me to travel with you."

"What kind of object?"

"The best one is something that has meaning to both of us, but anything of mine should work."

"Great! Where's your stuff?" Most of the furniture upstairs originally belonged to my grandfather, but I couldn't exactly lug the couch around town.

In response, he waved one hand. A trunk appeared in the corner, nearly identical to the one in my bedroom upstairs. Walter moved in front of it and waited, so I lifted that lid first.

The smell of cedar touched my nose, along with what must have been my grandfather's personal scent. As a ghost, he didn't smell like anything, but now I inhaled pine and something vaguely citrusy. Although I'd expected it to be packed with belongings, there were only two items: a necklace and a piece of paper.

"You needed an entire trunk for this?"

"I'm not about to show you all my goodies at once," he replied.

"It's spelled," Pink said, as though it was obvious. Maybe it should have been, but this was all still new to me.

"Right. Sorry."

First, I pulled out the necklace: a braided chain that somehow looked delicate and felt sturdy. Probably more magic. A gold heart pendant glinted in the low light. Wait, not a pendant. A hinge on one side told me that it was a locket. I pressed around until a hidden catch released and it fell open in my palm.

On the right, a man who actually did somewhat resemble Marlon Brando smiled out at me. Guess I shouldn't have been so skeptical. "You were a good-looking man, Walter."

"Told you so."

"Guess it runs in the family." The woman on the left looked so much like me that it took my breath away for a moment. "Grandma."

"That's right. I gave this locket to Vera when I asked her to marry me." He paused. "She gave it back the day she returned to your grandfather."

Once again, I wanted to reach out and offer some physical comfort, but my hand just went right through his. Goosebumps rose up my arm.

"I'm so sorry," I said.

"If the spell works, no need to apologize."

His mention of a spell reminded me of the piece of paper inside the trunk. I pulled it out and skimmed the words.

It required a few more steps than the spells I'd attempted so far. As I read the recipe out loud, each of them appeared in the bottom of the trunk: incense, a small cauldron, several candles, wooden matches, a bag of salt, and a packet of herbs.

"Neat trick," I said as I pulled the items out. "Can you teach me how to do that?"

"All things in time," Walter replied.

"Should we do it here?" I asked.

"You should not," Pink said. "If anything goes wrong, your grandfather would be stuck not just in this house but in the basement forever. Possibly with the two of us."

"Yikes."

"Let's do the ballroom," Walter said. "It's my favorite."

The three of us trooped upstairs, where I gathered everything together. First, Walter went to the center of the room. I drew a circle of salt around the two of us, while Pink moved over to sit on the piano bench.

"You're not helping."

"The last thing I want is to have to go everywhere you wear a necklace," he said. "I'm staying out of range."

"Fair enough."

Once the circle was complete, I placed candles around the circle. The locket went into the cauldron, which I set in the exact middle of the circle. Then I lit them. When that was finished, I sat cross-legged in front of the cauldron and read the words of the spell aloud.

The words were unfamiliar, yet speaking them felt right. This was nothing like my failed attempts at Wicca as a child. When I reached the end of the page, something moved through me. A whoosh of energy.

But when I looked up, everything appeared exactly the same.

"Did it work?" I asked, trying not to sound disappointed. "You don't look any different."

"I feel a little tingle," he said. "Are you sure you did it right?"

"How should I know? Hold on." I skimmed the spell again before holding it up. "According to this, it'll take about an hour for the full effect to hit. We can't go anywhere yet."

"Well, then, I guess we should go back to the basement. Go through the old memories together." He led the way into the darkness, but this time, I flipped the switch at the top of the stairs. Much better.

Now two trunks sat in the corner instead of one.

"Are you sure about this?" I asked.

"I'm sure. It's been a long time since I could physically go through my memories. Now we can do it together."

Reaching out my hand, I grasped where his hand would have been. He cackled. "Well, that's overly optimistic, but I appreciate the gesture."

When the lid of the first trunk creaked open, a blue and white crocheted blanket lay folded neatly on top.

"Frank made me that," Walter said.

"Your lawyer?"

"A man can have hobbies."

True enough, so I turned my attention back to the trunk. Under the blanket was a stack of photo albums. For some reason, I hadn't expected that, but Walter died long before smartphones were invented. He'd need to store pictures somewhere. With great care, I lifted the first one out and opened it.

An hour later, I sat back on my heels. We'd pored over the entire trove of pictures, spending time going over the detail of each one before moving on to the next. Many of them came with stories. I couldn't believe how much I looked like Grandma when she was younger. Also, as much as I hated to admit it, the Brando resemblance wasn't entirely in Walter's head. To my surprise, he also had baby pictures of my mother, some of them with her mother and the man she'd known as her father.

When we finally replaced everything in the trunk for safekeeping, tears blurred my vision.

"You really miss her, don't you?" Walter asked.

I nodded and sniffled. "She was my favorite person. I miss her every day."

"Me, too," he said. "Do you think you could do me a favor?"

"Um, sure. How can I help a ghost?"

"I want you to get my baseball glove."

I blinked several times. "I'm sorry—what?"

"A few weeks before my death, I loaned my auto-graphed Babe Ruth glove to Toby Grant. The next-door neighbor."

"Yeah, I know Toby. Unfortunately."

"He's not all bad. He's just stubborn. He'll warm up to you eventually."

"I appreciate your faith in humanity, but no way are we becoming friends."

Walter snorted. "Forget being friends with Toby. I want my glove. It's one-of-a-kind. Priceless. Should be in the Hall of Fame, that one. But it's not, because it was in my private collection. Toby asked if he could show his son, so I said okay. But then I died, and that son of a gun never brought it back. Probably planned on me kicking it before I could him to return my most prized possession."

I couldn't believe my ears. He was holding up a murder investigation for this? "You do realize it's been twenty-five years?"

"Twenty-six. The glove's worth even more now," he

ADA BELL

retorted. "Watch it, or I won't let you sell it once you bring it back."

"You're dead!" I put my hands on my hips. "Why would I even go ask for the glove if you want me to sell it? Neither of us needs the money."

"That was a test. Congratulations, you passed. Your grandmother got me that glove, and I want it."

"If we do this, will you help me find a spell to locate Martha's killer?"

"If you don't get it, I certainly won't."

That wasn't exactly the agreement I'd hoped for. It took all my restraint not to roll my eyes. With a dead cook, a closed bed-and-breakfast, and no ability to reopen until this thing was resolved, I didn't have time to deal with a hostile neighbor. Unfortunately, I didn't have a better way to figure things out.

A heavy sigh escaped me. "Let's go."

CHAPTER
SIXTEEN

The one and only time I'd been inside Toby's bed-and-breakfast was the day we met. He'd been perfectly pleasant until asking what I planned to do with Walter's house.

Amazing how fast a person could turn on you. As soon as I mentioned it was much too big for one person and I wanted to let out rooms temporarily, he'd become icy cold. I'd been shown out the door before you could say, "Maybe we could help each other."

It took a lot of deep breathing and yoga stretches before I talked myself into going back to a home where I knew with utter certainty I wasn't wanted. Well, not by the older owner. His son probably wouldn't mind saying hello.

To say Walter was excited to tag along would be the understatement of the century. He skipped along ahead of me, alternating between letting out cheers and whistling a jaunty tune. At one point, he held his arms out to the sides and twirled, face tilted to the sun. No matter how this venture turned out, it was worth it to see him so happy.

"How far can you go?" I called through the woods.

"Let's see!" He took off. I continued down the path, but whatever the answer, he could at least move out of my sight. Hopefully, he hadn't bounced back to the house.

When I arrived at Toby's, Walter waited on the steps, bouncing up and down. "Come on, Slowpoke!"

I choked back a laugh. "How far did you get?"

"Only here," he grumbled. "Probably farther now that you've caught up. Cover me, I'm going in!"

"I thought you were my backup," I said.

"Backup" was a bit of an overstatement. He wouldn't be useful if Toby chose to bodily remove me from the premises, but I appreciated the sentiment. It was nice to know I had someone on my side, even if he was invisible to everyone else.

Sorry, to everyone else other than the cat.

"Right." Walter bowed gallantly and gestured toward the door. "After you."

To my surprise, it wasn't Toby waiting behind the counter when I walked in but Cliff. If I'd considered the possibility of Toby not being there, I wouldn't have been nearly so hesitant to come over.

He greeted me with a smile. "Looking for a room? The police didn't kick you out of your outbuildings, too, did they?"

"As if I'd stay here after the way your dad stole my mitt then treated my granddaughter like garbage," Walter muttered under his breath. I loved that he felt the need to regulate his tone, despite knowing Cliff wouldn't hear even if he shouted.

I shook my head. "It feels weird living behind the mansion, but no. I'm allowed to stay. But I had to cancel all my guests."

"That must be tough, especially for a new business. You've barely had time to open."

Walter coughed. You'd think someone who'd been dead for twenty-six years would be more patient.

"It's just a minor setback," I said, eager to get to the point of why we were here. "Listen, I was looking for your dad. I've been going through some of my grandfather's things in storage. His lawyer, Frank, gave me an inventory of all the items belonging to the estate, and there's this old baseball glove signed by Babe Ruth, from when he used to pitch."

"Oh, yeah? That's so cool!"

"It is! Really, it should be in a museum somewhere. But according to the lawyer's records, it's here."

"What?" Cliff blinked at me.

"As if you don't know," Walter said.

"Apparently, my grandfather loaned it to your dad before he died, and no one ever came to get it back." I held one hand up to stop his protests. "I know what you're thinking. What right do I have to ask for a priceless piece of baseball history after all this time? None. But it seems like it was really important to my grandfather, and I'm hoping you'd be willing to return it."

"Tell you what, girlie," Toby said from the doorway. "You close your bed-and-breakfast; you can have the glove. Free."

Cliff whirled toward him. "You told me that glove belonged to you!"

"It is mine," he retorted. "It's not like the Babe is going to walk down from Heaven and ask to use it. Neither is 'ole Brando, for that matter."

"Don't be so sure," Walter said.

My lips twitched, but I forced myself to ignore him.

"Dad, you know that's not fair," Cliff said.

I was very relieved to have him on my side. Yes, I could buy the glove from Toby, but he seemed the type to refuse to sell solely out of spite. More likely, I was going to have to do a locator spell to figure out where he'd hidden it, then steal the thing.

Unfortunately, I didn't actually know how to do that yet. That plan would also mean erasing both Toby's memory and Cliff's. Which I also didn't know how to do. Really, I should have started with a locator spell. No one would have suspected me if the glove vanished before they knew I wanted it. What kind of witch was I?

Well, maybe I was a decent witch, yet a bad law-breaker. I could live with that.

The two men engaged in a silent staring contest. Despite Toby's obvious advantage as the father, Cliff seemed to be winning.

After what felt like forever but was probably about forty-five seconds, Toby muttered something under his breath, then broke eye contact with his son. He glared at us both from the doorway, then stomped out. He returned a few minutes later, carrying a glass box display case. The glove sat inside. "The box is mine, you know. You'll have to leave it."

"Don't get your finger oils on my glove!" Walter said behind me.

"I will happily reimburse you for the box," I said. "I'd rather keep the glove as pristine as it is now."

"Payment won't be necessary," Cliff said, glaring at his father over my head. "Consider it rent for all the time we've been holding onto your possession."

"Thank you."

"Why are you still here? You got what you wanted. Now

go." To Cliff, Toby said, "Lunch is in ten minutes. Don't be late because you're busy flirting with the girl who's trying to steal our business."

"Flirting, eh?" Walter elbowed me. "There something you want to tell me? You could do a lot worse. He's got great bone structure."

Never did I think I'd be talking to my dead grandfather about my love life. Good thing I couldn't speak until we got outside.

My cheeks flamed. A glance at Cliff showed me that his cheeks were as red as mine. He was very good-looking when he blushed. Neither of us said a word as Toby stomped off down the hall. To my great amusement, Walter followed, making faces at his back. "Boo!"

I didn't even try to hide the smile. Let Cliff think I was amused by the "flirting" comment. I liked the guy, and I thought he might like me, too. Why hide it? At forty-two, I wasn't getting any younger.

Maybe this was a terrible time to start a relationship. Maybe it was inappropriate to flirt while investigating a murder. But you couldn't always help where love found you, and if I'd learned anything, it was that life was too short not to grab things that might make us happy. As soon as I found Martha's killer and cleared Josie's name, I'd be back to invite him to dinner.

Once Toby was out of earshot, I turned back to Cliff. "Thank you. I know it seems weird, but I really want something to help me feel closer to my grandfather. This entire week has been awful, and I thought it would help."

"I understand. The other morning, I sensed you didn't want to talk about the details of what happened, but I'm here for you when you're ready."

"I appreciate that, but I'm okay."

"Is it true that you found her?" When I nodded, he reached over and squeezed my hand. "I'm sorry."

"Did you know Martha?" I asked.

"Of course I did," he said. "Martha's lived here forever. I think she moved to the area after her husband died. Wow, that's over twenty years."

"I thought she was in the military?"

"She was, but there's a base near Saratoga. Naval Support."

It hadn't occurred to me she might have been stationed in the area. When people mentioned Saratoga, I thought about horse racing, not the military. "You don't know anyone who would want to kill her, do you?"

"Would you believe no one mentioned it?"

"Yes, unfortunately."

Cliff leaned across the counter and lowered his voice. "Here's what I know. First, she made the most amazing cinnamon rolls I've ever had in my life. We used to go to the County Fair just to buy some. Dad wanted to serve those here. Second, there was definitely some tension with her kids after she moved in with them. I don't think she liked her daughter-in-law very much."

If television was to be believed, no one liked their in-laws. But family conflict was as good a starting point as any when looking for a motive.

I thanked him and turned to leave, but he called me back. "Emma?"

"Yeah?"

"Oooh, I know what's happening now." Walter reappeared in that unsettling way of his and winked at me. "Go get 'em, girl."

Before I could protest that this was a perfectly innocent conversation, he vanished.

Cliff was still gazing at me, concern growing with each second I remained silent. "Are you okay?"

With effort, I swallowed. "Yeah, I think so. This whole thing is so difficult. I was just thinking, what if I had been the one in the kitchen?"

"Don't think like that," Cliff said. "Blaming yourself for being alive or worrying about what ifs is the road to misery."

"Thanks." I held his gaze for a moment, trying to convey more than just gratitude. It might have been my imagination, but I thought I saw my conflicted emotions reflected in his eyes.

Upstairs, a door slammed. We both jumped.

Cliff ran a hand through his hair, mussing it in a way that somehow made him even better-looking. With a glance at the ceiling, he said, "Listen, I have to fix a squeaky hinge on the bathroom door upstairs. But if you need me, you can call anytime."

"Thanks." I held up the glove. "I should get this back. Add it to my inventory."

"No problem."

There wasn't any reason to linger, but I took an inordinately long amount of time to walk across the lobby to the front door. My hand was on the knob when Cliff's voice finally stopped me. "If you really want to thank me, maybe you could go to dinner with me sometime. There's this great Indian place nearby."

A huge smile crossed my face. "I'd like that."

Five minutes later, after a trip through the tunnel that seemed much longer when carrying a big glass box, I made it back to the ballroom. Now, how to summon my grandfather? He seemed to pop up whenever and wherever he wanted. Could he hear me? Was he watching where I couldn't see him? Maybe he'd been silently cheering for me and Cliff, then followed me all the way home.

I wasn't sure how all of this worked, but he couldn't go too far from the house. He wouldn't have just popped over to the Babe Ruth exhibit at Cooperstown.

"Walter?" I called softly, even though no one could be in the house to hear me.

Nothing.

I went to the piano and sat, running my hands over the keys. My last piano lesson was in 1986, so I hoped my grandfather liked *Heart & Soul*. Maybe if he heard the music, he'd realize I was back and come see me. Just in case, I set the glass case on the bench next to me before putting my hands on the keys.

"There you are!" he said, appearing at my elbow. "Did you get a date?"

My cheeks flamed. "That's none of your business."

"You did! Why don't you seem happier?"

"I'm thrilled," I ground out. "There's nothing I love more than running errands for my dead grandfather when I should be solving a murder. Here's the glove."

"Thank you! That's so wonderful!!" Walter clapped his hands together gleefully. In some ways, he reminded me of a child. Or maybe he'd just been so bored living alone as a ghost for thirty years that literally every interaction was exciting. A bit of my irritation evaporated. "Now we can go to a game!"

This was not the response I'd expected. "A game? You said you just wanted the glove back."

"Of course I wanted it back. It's nearly priceless. But now we can go on an outing! Oh, this will be so much fun."

"Okay, hold on. First, you are aware that Babe Ruth has

been dead for about a hundred years, right? We can't watch him play unless you've got tickets to the afterlife."

"You don't know. Maybe I do," he grumbled.

"If you did, you wouldn't need me to make you a magic necklace," I pointed out reasonably.

"I don't need you!" he said.

"Great! Go to a game. See you later."

He slumped against the side of the piano. "Okay, I was bluffing."

What a sad life. Decades of haunting your own empty house, then having to wait for your granddaughter to take you places. Mentally, I added buying theater tickets to my list of things to do when this was all over.

"The afterlife sure isn't all it's cracked up to be, is it?" I asked.

"Oh, it's lovely for a lot of people. Most people move on once they've resolved their unfinished business. Some people have no regrets, like Martha. They move on instantly. But I wanted to meet you, to help guide you. This was the best way."

"The absolute best, huh? You couldn't have popped in to say hi while I was in college?"

"I didn't know where you were," he said. "You think I set up a treasure hunt for my health? It's all part of the legacy: the house, the magic, the talking cat, and the ability to interact with me."

That got me thinking. "Can I see all ghosts?"

"I don't know. I can see other ghosts. When Martha arrived, I was here. I don't know whether you'd be able to see another spirit if I wasn't with you. Everyone's power is different."

"Not sure how I would test that. Walking around looking for ghosts seems like a poor life choice."

He nodded. "Not all ghosts are friendly. I'd suggest finding another way to test your powers. Tell you what, if there are any ghosts at the baseball game, I'll move away and you let me know if you still see them."

I snorted. "Way to bring it back around."

"You didn't think you were getting out of this, did you? I've been stuck in the house for twenty-six years with no one but the cat to talk to."

"I heard that," Pink said, making me jump. Until he spoke, I hadn't realized he was here. "I happen to be a brilliant conversationalist."

"Yeah, you're a rock star. Really, more of a pop star. You cover me in sunshine. But Emma is my flesh and blood."

Walter was as good as my mom at the guilt trips. Maybe she inherited that ability from him. "Fine. Let me check their schedule. But after, we've got to start practicing my magic."

"What's the rush? She'll be just as dead tomorrow."

Although that was technically true, it missed the point. "I want to move forward and start my new life here. I can't do that with a murder hanging over me."

"Yeah, yeah. I get it. But you found a dead body yesterday, and you need to have some fun."

His point could not be refuted. Taking one night away probably wouldn't make the difference between finding Martha's killer and not. Although I didn't particularly want to go, I didn't have a good reason to say no. He wasn't going to teach me any spells if we stayed.

If only I'd moved in during the winter, it may have been possible to avoid this outing. Unfortunately, it was not only a beautiful August day, but the Valley Cats were in town and playing in just a couple of hours. And since my ghostly grandfather could read as well as I could, all this information became available to him by peeking over my shoulder at my phone.

Oops.

Note to self: conduct stealthy recon mission in the bathroom next time.

"There! Seven o'clock! We've got time!" His excitement made him louder with each word, until I would have agreed to almost anything to get him to lower the volume.

I heaved a heavy sigh. "Let's go."

There was no reasonable way to explain to Josie that, in the midst of a murder investigation centering on our home, a victim we'd both known, and the police targeting at least one of us as a potential killer, I'd decided to jaunt down to Albany for a baseball game because my ghostly grandfather demanded it. Unfortunately, the game was what Walter wanted, and he wouldn't help me until I took him. The books were helpful, but nothing compared to a real, live mentor.

Or a real, dead mentor, as the case may be.

After spending too much time trying to come up with an excuse, I decided to simply invite Josie to go with me. We'd been through a lot, the property held bad vibes, and I wanted a night of happy outdoor memories to clear the air. I thought she might not want to be home alone.

Either Josie bought the lie or she wanted a free dinner, because she agreed to join me with very little persuading.

I absolutely refused to explain to my passenger that Walter wanted to sit in the front seat, so Josie climbed in beside me. My grandfather moved through the rear door and slid into the middle seat in a way that made the hair on my arms stand up. Although ghosts on television often walked through solid objects, it wasn't something I'd

ADA BELL

expected to ever witness. Just another thing to get used to now.

Emma, we're not in Kansas anymore.

Once we buckled up, I checked the mirror. Walter sat back against the seat, arms folded across his seat, looking like the human embodiment of Grumpy Cat.

When we got to the game, though, I had no choice but to buy a third, empty seat. Water refused to stand, and I didn't want him sitting on my lap.

Josie shot me a questioning look. "Is someone joining us? Maybe that contractor I saw flirting with you?"

My cheeks grew warm. "No, um, when I was a kid, I used to go to games with my grandpa. I wanted to buy him a seat so I feel like he's here with us."

"Nice save, kid," Walter said.

"You're kind of weird, you know that?" she said.

"I'm weird, but I'm buying your ticket and dinner," I said.

"Don't get me wrong. I like weird."

"Me, too," I said with a smile.

When we took our seats, I put the one beside me down and set a baseball glove from the basement on it. Not the priceless collector's glove, just one that Pink pulled out of a trunk for me. Walter settled onto the spot with a big smile. Somehow, he'd gotten a Valley Cats cap to wear.

As weird as this whole thing felt, the big smile on his face for the next nine innings convinced me I'd done the right thing.

Josie was happy, too. Especially when they came by with a t-shirt cannon, and I used my magic to persuade one of the Valley Cats t-shirts into her outstretched hands. This outing did wonders for both of us.

Unfortunately, our happiness was short-lived.

The lights in both cottages blazed when we turned into the driveway of the mansion about an hour after the game ended. We'd left in the middle of the afternoon, so the windows should have been dark.

"Did you leave your lights on?" I asked Josie.

"No, I don't think so."

That was rather unsettling.

"Are you expecting anyone?"

"Nope."

My first instinct was to throw the car in reverse and stomp on the accelerator. Get out of Dodge. Instead, I lifted my foot off the pedal and allowed the car to creep up the driveway, while scouring the area for another vehicle. Anyone who parked off in the woods somewhere should definitely be avoided.

There. On the far side of the mansion, over by the barn, sat a dark-colored sedan. If I wasn't mistaken, it was the same one Detective Pratt drove.

Jinkies.

"Coppers!" Walter yelled as if this was an old TV show. "Hide!"

Unfortunately, that wasn't an option for the humans in the car. While my ghostly grandfather dove through the trunk lid, Josie and I had fewer viable options.

"Do I have any missed calls?" I asked.

She picked up my phone and pressed a button. "No. Why—oh."

I realized the second she spotted the police car, too. If the police had arrested another suspect, they would have called before dropping by. If they needed to get back in the mansion, he would have called as a courtesy and also so I could open the doors for them.

An unannounced visit from the police officer investigating Martha's death could not be a good thing. I didn't even touch the brakes, just keep rolling forward while searching for any positive outcome. Eventually, the car stopped.

"You've got this," Josie said. "Everything will be okay."

I squeezed her hand. "Thanks. You, too."

As we got out of the car, the door to Josie's cottage swung inward. Detective Pratt came out onto the stoop.

"Dios me," she muttered under her breath.

"Look at the bright side. At least nothing could get stolen with the police here." Louder, I said, "Hi, Detective. Not to be rude, but you're not allowed to walk into the cottages. That's not part of the crime scene. That was our deal, remember? I vacate the main house, you let me stay on the premises?"

"Yes, I remember that conversation," he said. "But in this case, I have a warrant."

Yikes. My mouth went dry. With great difficulty, I forced myself to ask. "Okay, then. How can I help you?"

His lips pressed firmly into a line before he handed me a piece of paper. A chill went down my spine. Whatever he was about to tell me, I didn't think I was going to like it. "I was looking for the two of you."

"Do you need to search the mansion again?" I asked, wondering how to explain his total aversion to entering my bedroom. I'd have to either go with him or figure out—quickly—how to lift the spell for an hour or so. "Give me a minute, and I'll let you in. Next time, call first and you won't have to wait.

He shook his head. "No, I'm not here to search. The DNA test results came back. Josie Ross, you're under arrest for the murder of Martha Armstrong."

CHAPTER
SEVENTEEN

Asob escaped me at Detective Pratt's proclamation. I couldn't believe this was happening. I wanted to run at him, beg him to change his mind. Insist that it must have been anyone else, that Josie absolutely had nothing to do with Martha's death. I involuntarily took a step forward, but she put a hand on my arm.

"Don't. I'll be okay."

"But you're innocent."

"I have faith that justice will prevail," she said. "Don't get yourself in trouble for me. Once they take me away, you can reopen your business."

"My business isn't nearly as important as my friend's freedom."

Before she could respond, Detective Pratt cleared his throat. "If it's all the same to you, Emma, I need to read Mrs. Ross her rights."

My heart sank at that. They had made their decision. Detective Pratt wouldn't be swayed by anything I said right now. The best thing I could do to help Josie was hire someone to defend her, then figure out who really did this. I stepped back, out of the way. "Josie, I'll come visit as soon as I can. I'll talk to my grandfather's lawyer."

She smiled a sad thank you before being led away.

Over his shoulder, Detective Pratt said, "I know you hate me right now, but all the evidence points this way. Her DNA was on the murder weapon."

"I told you she wore that apron on Monday!"

He continued as if I hadn't spoken, "The good news is, you're free to return to the main house."

A steely glare was my only response.

I stood on the path, watching while Detective Pratt loaded my friend into the car. Since I hadn't been able to protect Josie from the charges, I owed it to her to witness the results. The taillights turned out of sight at the end of the driveway before I allowed myself to walk away.

Although I should have been tired enough to fall asleep immediately, I was too stressed to even climb into bed. What evidence could have led them to arrest Josie? Her fingerprints couldn't have been on the rings. She wouldn't have confessed, and I'd already explained that her DNA got on the apron during her job interview. I couldn't believe the police still thought she was guilty.

She needed a lawyer, fast. The only one I knew was Walter's old estate lawyer. He'd actually been retired except for finalizing the distribution of my grandfather's assets, and I didn't imagine Frank would take on a criminal case now that he was completely done. He also wouldn't appreciate me calling at this hour, but I did it, anyway.

Straight to voicemail. His cell phone was off. I left a message asking him to refer me to a criminal lawyer in the morning, then paced my small cottage, examining the evidence from every angle.

When that failed me, I pored over my spell books until I

fell asleep. Pink jumped onto the couch and hustled me off to bed, where I was pretty sure he spelled me to sleep. I was too worn out to complain, but he'd get an earful later.

The next morning, although I desperately wanted to see Walter and see if he could teach me a useful spell, I went to Martha's funeral instead. For one thing, I could speak with her daughter-in-law. Martha had left me a message to pass on, and I'd been too preoccupied to do it.

Besides, someone there might have some idea what happened. I needed to figure this out as soon as possible. The whole point of opening up Walter's home to the public was to help people. Instead of helping Josie, she was in jail. To date, my endeavor was a total failure.

Although I didn't have many clothes that would be funeral-appropriate, it didn't take much magic to coax a pair of my black pants into becoming a knee-length skirt instead. Pink's revelation that Dottie couldn't tell when I did magic made me much more confident. A few minor alterations to my red t-shirt, well, let's just say it was quite different when I finished.

After a quick makeup application, I slid my feet into a pair of sandals glamoured to look like high heels and headed for my car. Halfway there, I paused.

Should I take Walter with me? He was so lonely. Might want to see some people he used to know. But funerals were a solemn affair. He'd probably be bored to tears. He'd also be distracting when I needed to speak to Martha's daughter-in-law about the recipe. Or he might make me miss her entirely.

After a moment, I went into the ballroom and asked.

Walter looked aghast. "Me? Attend a funeral? Oh, no! I hated doing that when I was alive."

"You don't want to be around more people?"

"I spent last night in a baseball stadium. I'm good. Oh, that reminds me. You said you could turn on any show I wanted, right? Before you go, can you turn on a game?"

"Sure? If I can find one. It's early, but sometimes they show historic games."

In the time it took me to find what he wanted to watch, Walter changed into a baseball jersey and Yankee's hat. He perched on the couch. "Before you go, can I have my glove?"

"What about the destructive oils on my fingers?"

"Don't open the box, just put it on the couch."

"Okay, but when I get back, it's magic time."

"Yeah, yeah." He rolled his eyes. "You're awfully demanding for someone I made a millionaire."

Instead of responding, I headed for my car. I wasn't sure where the funeral home was, and if I didn't leave soon, I'd be late. Walking into a stranger's funeral after it started wasn't a good look.

Unfortunately, when I opened the door to my little Corolla, the interior light didn't come on. Weird, but I'd deal with it later. After pulling up the address on my phone, I put the key in the ignition and turned it.

Nothing happened.

With a frown, I turned it again.

Click. Click. Click.

Uh-oh.

I pumped the accelerator, because I'd heard once that could do something. Once again, the car refused to start.

"Wonderful. What else can possibly go wrong?"

Pulling out my phone, I did a quick search that confirmed my suspicion: the battery was dead. Not completely shocking because it was at least five years old. Still, terrible timing. I didn't have time to get a new one, or a way to get to the auto parts store. I also didn't know where the nearest auto part store was or how to install a battery.

Cliff. Cliff would know. I could call him and ask. Although I hated looking like a damsel in distress, if the trope fits...

While I was trying to talk myself into exercising my only legitimate option, no matter how pathetic it made me look, a familiar shiny red BMW convertible turned into the driveway. Great. The last person I wanted to deal with right now was driving up to the mansion. Maybe if I slid down in my seat, she wouldn't see me. It seemed futile, but I was in enough of a mood to give it a shot.

Three seconds later, a honking horn made me jump.

Looking up, I found Dottie stopped beside me. Her window rolled down. When I just stared, she gestured for me to do the same.

Argh!

"That's a nice outfit. Where did you get it?"

"My closet."

She laughed. "Nice try. I can see the sheen of magic on the clothes, my dear."

Pink may have failed to mention that minor fact. Traitor. But since I was caught, it wasn't worth pretending anymore.

"Are you mad at me?" I asked.

"Mad isn't the right word. Disappointed that you don't seem to have taken our earlier chat to heart. And I will need to have another chat with your familiar. If Pink can't help guide you, then maybe he doesn't need to be here."

"Pink told me you lied about being able to detect my magic," I said pointedly. "He just didn't mention you would see the residue."

"He doesn't know all my secrets," she said.

"Well, you'll be glad to know he's been helping, even if it's not in the direction you wanted. I've been practicing, honing my skills. Not suppressing my magic and pretending it doesn't exist."

"I don't want you to pretend it doesn't exist," she said. "That could have disastrous results. I just didn't want you to use magic constantly, to rely on it for things you could do yourself. Especially flashy magic like remodeling a house! It's okay to do a minor spell here and there."

"You couldn't have mentioned that sooner?"

"No. You needed to learn discretion and control."

"Fine, I get it. But I have to go. Martha's funeral service starts soon."

"I know. I'll go with you."

I wasn't about to give her time to think about the offer in case she changed her mind. Grabbing my purse, I climbed out of my car and into hers in a heartbeat. "You drive."

Seconds later, we were on the road. Weird how navigating the driveway took so much longer and felt so much bumpier in my car.

"Your grandfather was a hearth witch, too, you know. His magic was the strongest in the home. He did all sorts of things with thread. Won the knitting bee every year, the cheater."

I snorted. "Sounds like Walt. Is that why he got stuck in the house? Because his magic is tied to the home?"

The mansion was nice and all, but I didn't relish the thought of living there for all eternity with my cranky grandfather's ghost and a talking cat.

She shook her head. "Not exactly. That's not important. What is important is that he should have left you a spell book."

"He did. I don't think he used it much. A lot of it is blank."

"It's not blank, it's protected. Any spell you're not ready to use won't show up."

"That's what Pink said," I grumbled.

"Have you tried the early spells, the ones you can see?"

"Yeah. I was using them to make my new house look awesome, and then some cranky MEOW lady showed up and told me to stop."

Her lips twitched. "It wasn't *stop* so much as *slow down*."

"Then why are you here?"

"I guessed you would want to go to Martha's funeral. Since you won't know anyone, I thought you'd feel more comfortable if we went together."

The unexpected gesture warmed my heart. Maybe I wasn't quite as friendless as I thought. I smiled at her awkwardly. "Oh. Well, thanks for caring."

"I didn't say I cared." So much for our touching moment. She cleared her throat as she parked. "You're my responsibility. If you try spells you're not ready for and make a mess of it, I'll have to run around doing memory wipes. Nobody has time for that. Come on, the service is starting."

People were packed into the funeral home, filling seats from one wall to the other. I felt oddly touched to see the crowd. Even though she was a bit prickly, all these people showed up at Martha's funeral to say goodbye. It was nice to see the way the town came together. If I died, it would just be a cat, a ghost, and three people from the next town over. Maybe Cliff.

We'd barely managed to push our way inside when a well-built man with silver hair and an air of authority stepped up to the podium at the front of the room and gestured for silence. The chatter stopped. "Thank you, everyone, for coming today. I know Martha's family appreciates it."

Behind me, someone muttered, "Martha wouldn't have."

The man at the front didn't even pause. "If you'll all take your seats, we're going to start in just a minute."

I met Dottie's eyes, and she tilted her head slightly behind me. She'd also heard the comment. Together, we trailed behind the women we believed to have spoken. I was prepared to sit behind or next to her, but I didn't expect her to go all the way to the front row and sit behind a somber man wearing Martha's exact features. Whoever she was, she appeared to be very pregnant.

"That must be her daughter-in-law," I muttered to Dottie as we found two seats near the back. "My neighbor told me they didn't get along."

She glanced over. "Yeah, that's Darlene. Her husband Mark is on the left. Wonder who they got to watch the kids."

Right. I'd forgotten Dottie lived here and knew everyone. I was about to ask for more dirt on the family when the funeral director started to speak again.

The service was lovely, yet uneventful. No one stood up to confess to killing Martha. All of the eulogies were respectful. Some were even funny. The daughter-in-law didn't give a eulogy, just sat and stared straight ahead.

When everyone streamed out at the end, I didn't know any more than when we arrived. This was starting to feel like a waste of time. But I had a mission. Martha wanted me to pass a message to Darlene, and I would do it before heading home. She was easy enough to find, considering her slow gait and large belly. On the other side of the room, she spoke with a man whose features mirrored Martha's. Must have been another son. He leaned forward and kissed her cheek. Then she walked away alone, moving toward the swinging door that servers had been carrying food through.

With a deep breath, I followed Darlene. This was the first time she'd been alone since I arrived. It was now or never.

EIGHTEEN

W hen I followed Darlene through the swinging doors into the kitchen, she was alone. She leaned against a counter, face in her hands, breathing hard. I desperately hoped she wasn't going into early labor.

There was no point in beating around the bush. I didn't know Martha's daughter-in-law, didn't have any other way of reaching her, and didn't particularly want to search out her address to show up at her house unannounced. This was my chance to convey Martha's message. Direct and to the point, just like her mother-in-law would have wanted.

Clearing my throat, I approached.

When Darlene looked at me, her eyes narrowed. "I'm sorry, but this is a private area. Funeral guests aren't allowed in the kitchen."

"This won't take long. I just need a moment of your time. I've, uh, got a message for you."

"Who are you?"

"I'm Emma. It was my place where..." There was no good way to say it. "I'm very sorry for your loss."

"The bed-and-breakfast owner?" When I nodded, she said, "Martha told me about you! I'm Darlene, but you know that already. You're the one who found her."

"Yes, unfortunately."

"I wish you hadn't overheard me complaining before the service, but my mother-in-law and I weren't close. She didn't think I was good enough for her 'little boy.' Who was, by the way, thirty when we got married."

There was definitely no love lost between Martha and her daughter-in-law. Sure, the older woman handed over the recipe after her death, but at the moment, Darlene topped my suspect list. She didn't like her mother-in-law. Martha had refused to give Darlene something she'd wanted, and she wasn't sorry the woman was dead. She also knew where to find Martha before she died, and killing her outside the home might have been her way of deflecting suspicion.

Motive, opportunity. She'd found the means on site. The pieces all fit. If only I had a way to prove it.

Alas, I was here to resolve some unfinished business. Whether or not Darlene killed her, Martha had asked me to relay a message, and I would. Until there was some hard evidence pointing in Darlene's direction, I owed it to Martha. If Darlene was guilty, she couldn't make cinnamon rolls in jail, anyway.

"On Tuesday morning, Martha was making her cinnamon rolls. She told me all they won first prize at the fair so many years in a row, and that you loved them. She said everyone was clamoring for the recipe."

Darlene eyed me suspiciously. "Yes, they were. Everyone. That recipe was top secret. She never even let anyone in the kitchen when she was making them. Never. So what were you doing there?"

Oops. I knew that, too. Martha had thrown a fit when Josie wandered in, accused her of trying to steal the secret ingredient. "Um, the dough was already mixed. She was letting it rest. Er, rise. Anyway, she said she was ready to hand over the reins, let you make them for family gatherings. I don't know if she got a chance to tell you, but she wanted you to know the recipe is on a card hidden in the bottom drawer of her jewelry box. The key is inside an old pill bottle in her bathroom. Look for one that's expired."

Darlene gasped. "No. Are you serious?"

"I am. She adores her grandchildren, and she wanted to be sure they could enjoy her treats if anything happened to her. I'm sure she didn't think that day would come so soon."

"Why would she tell you this? No offense, but she didn't even know you."

"Sometimes it's easier to talk to a stranger." Especially when you're dead and no one else can hear you.

Darlene clutched my hand between both of hers and shook it. "Thank you! Thank you!"

I patted her shoulder awkwardly to comfort her. A few minutes later, her husband walked in. I took a long look at the man who had been Martha's son. He stood stiff as a board when the door opened, but when he spotted Darlene with me, he relaxed.

"Is she okay?" he asked.

Darlene turned into her husband's arms as I patted her back one more time.

"I think she will be," I said.

It was time to leave this poor family to their grief. I'd delivered Martha's message, and there was no need to stay.

Back in the main room, I found Dottie and explained that I'd prefer to make my own way back to the mansion. As

I thanked her for bringing me with her, I could've sworn a faint smile crossed her lips. She liked me, even if she didn't want to.

As I turned to leave, a familiar face caught my eye. In the center of all the activity, I spotted Thelma Reyes, Shady Grove's premier gossip. It surprised me to see her so far from home, but I supposed a good scandal was a good scandal, no matter where it happened.

Thelma used to star in my favorite soap opera, *As the Hospital Guides Our Lives.* When I was a kid, Grandma would come over when I was sick and watch it with me. Then, as I got older, she started recording it on her VCR and bringing me the tapes when Mom wasn't home. It was our secret. Thelma was an icon, a living legend. Suddenly, I wished I had something for her to autograph.

If anyone had the goods on Martha's enemies, it would be Thelma. I moved toward the crowd, trying to listen without calling too much attention to myself. Unfortunately, the woman was sharp as a tack and extremely observant: two things that made her an excellent gossip.

When I drew near, she looked up and spotted me instantly. "You there. Why do you look familiar?"

My plan to avoid drawing attention to myself went out the window when a few people sidled out of the way, clearing a path between me and Thelma. With a gulp, I moved toward her. "You're from Shady Grove, right? I won the Treasure Hunt last summer."

"Ah, yes. Twenty-six years of searching high and low, and a stranger solves the puzzle in one day. Impressive."

I couldn't help it. Pride made me beam. "Thanks."

"How did you do it?"

To be honest, I did it because the clues were spelled in a way that made it impossible for anyone other than Walter's heir to solve them. Deflection seemed the better option. "I played *Clue* a lot as a child. Terrible what happened to Martha, isn't it? Did you know her well?"

As if I'd uttered magic words, Thelma drew herself upright and touched a white silken handkerchief to one eye. "I don't know what I'll do without her. There is a hole in my life. Martha was like a sister to me."

The words should have made my heart go out to her, but they sounded rehearsed. Grandma and I watched approximately four thousand episodes if *As the Hospital Guides Our Lives* over the years. Thelma was one hundred percent in character. In fact, that speech might have been actually taken from an episode of the show.

Rather than confront her and make an enemy in front of the entire town, I said, "I'm so sorry for your loss. Do you know who could have done such a terrible thing?"

"Well, naturally, I wouldn't have any idea." She looked around with a smug smile. "But I do sometimes pick up a thing or two. People love to open up to me, you know. So I might have some *idea*. But I don't like to spread tall tales."

It took a lot of control to keep from snorting. Thelma told more tales than the *National Enquirer*. Even I knew that. More likely, she was looking for a little tit for tat.

Leaning in, I lowered my voice. "Martha was in my home when she died. I'm the one who found her. That's why I feel this responsibility to find out who did it."

Thelma gasped, placing one hand on her chest. "Oh, dear! That must have been so horrible for you."

"Yes. Tragic. I still can't believe it. I would give anything to know what happened to her."

"Oh, really? I might know a little something, but you can't tell a soul." There were still at least a dozen people within earshot, and Thelma's voice carried like a beacon.

But I nodded to encourage her. "I don't know if I should say anything, but a man who lives in the area told me he took a walk through the woods that morning. He swore he saw someone skulking around your property, headed toward the kitchen. Looking like she was trying not to be noticed."

Really? That brought me back to the counter. Maybe this person had seen the killer! "Who was it? I have this weird idea it might have been Martha's daughter-in-law. They apparently didn't get along, and I found Martha's wedding rings tossed aside in my yard. That seemed personal."

"I doubt it," she said. "As you saw, Darlene is very pregnant. Even at a distance most people would have recognized that. According to my source, this woman was short, with graying brown hair. Darker skin than you and me. She was walking hunched over, like she didn't want anyone to notice her. That's what seemed odd to him. Does she sound familiar at all?"

My heart pounded. Yes. Yes, that description very much did sound familiar.

Thelma's source saw Josie near the kitchen right before Martha got killed.

CHAPTER
NINETEEN

Thelma knew someone who spotted Josie outside the mansion right before Martha was killed. When Josie should have been in her room, packing. I needed to know who she'd talked to.

"Are you absolutely sure?"

"Positive."

"Who told you that?"

She widened her eyes, pretending to be scandalized. "My dear girl, I could never reveal my sources. What do you take me for?"

A talented actress. Attention seeker. Neither of which meant she was even telling the truth. Maybe I should have buttered her up by asking for an autograph before seeking information. Too late now. I thanked her and headed for the exit. It wasn't worth arguing that Josie was innocent if Thelma had decided otherwise.

Outside, I found a voicemail from Walter's lawyer telling me he'd asked a friend who practiced criminal law to go to the jail and speak with Josie. Excellent news. I decided to make made a quick detour before going home. The local bank should be open. I could get cash, swing by the police station, and bail Josie out.

How much cash? No idea.

How long did it take to get a bail hearing? No idea.

Okay, scratch the bank for now. Maybe Detective Pratt could tell me how much I'd need. I might be furious with him for arresting Josie, but he probably didn't know that. Or if he did, he could explain the bail system as a way of making it up to me. Not the best plan, but all I had at the moment. I wanted to do what I could to help Josie.

The police station wasn't far from the funeral home, so I said goodbye to Dottie and headed over on foot. The walk took seven minutes—not as long as I'd hoped to have to gather my courage, but stalling wouldn't make me feel better. I paused on the sidewalk outside, took a deep breath, and said a quick spell to get the wrinkles out of my clothes. There. Now I looked like I could handle anything.

Feigning confidence I didn't feel, I strode into the police department. This town was so small, part of me expected a setup like on *The Andy Griffith Show*. Just a desk on one side and a jail cell on the other. It was small, but not that small.

The inside of the brick building looked more like the interior of Dunder-Mifflin than the Mayberry jail. Just your regular office with a receptionist desk at the front and a handful of desks. Each one was equipped with a computer and phone, as expected. No handcuffs or guns lying around. No giant metal ring with one key hanging on a hook outside the wall to the jail.

An unsmiling receptionist called Detective Pratt to ask if he was willing to see me. A door behind me opened, and he came out of his office.

"Emma! What can I do for you?"

"I'm here to bail out Josie," I said.

"Sorry, Emma, I can't do that. There's no bail set. She has to go before the judge first."

Not to be deterred, I named a number. "I can have a cashier's check within the hour."

"Are you trying to bribe a police officer?" His dancing eyes told me he was joking. Probably. "Listen, I'm sorry you had to come all the way down here for nothing."

"What's the problem?"

"Two things. First, I can't set the bail for this type of case. She has to go to court and get arraigned. Second, most judges don't give bail in murder cases."

"But I've got money! I can vouch for her!" Wasn't being rich supposed to make life easier?

"Can you? I seem to remember the day we met, you went to fetch her to answer some questions, and she'd disappeared."

He had me there. My mind raced for a response. "Just a misunderstanding."

"Uh-huh. I'm sure it was."

"She came back," I pointed out. "And she spoke with you voluntarily."

He put his hands on his hips. "You're welcome to come to the courthouse this afternoon and make your case to the judge. The arraignment is at one. But I recommend you not offer her cash. Your money would be better spent paying a lawyer to defend Josie."

Hmmph.

"You didn't call her husband, did you?"

After looking around the room, he lowered his voice. "No, I didn't. We've told the press there's a suspect in custody, but haven't released the name. The chief wanted me to go over there, but I pulled some medical records instead."

My brow wrinkled. "Martha's?"

"No, Josie's. Based on what I saw, our next visit to Josie's husband may not be to sell tickets to the policeman's ball. He won't get any information about her whereabouts from me."

A wave of relief flooded me. "You're a good man, Detective."

"Thanks. Just doing my job. Which does *not* involve releasing murder suspects."

I sighed. "Can I at least talk to her?"

He glanced at his watch. "Twenty minutes. Then we have to do lunch so she can be processed and taken to the courthouse."

The courthouse was next door, so I didn't know how much processing time was needed, but I didn't argue. "Thank you."

Detective Pratt called a tall, willowy blond woman over and introduced her as Officer Peterson. Then he asked her to take me to see Josie. She nodded to him, gave me a once over, then walked away without waiting for me to follow. I hurried after her.

"How long have you been working here?"

She didn't reply.

Following her lead, I remained silent as we went through a door with many locks on it. Inside was a room very similar to the holding cells you see on TV. There were three separate cells, two of them occupied. A man lay on a bench in the far right cell, arm flung over his eyes. He appeared to be asleep. Josie was on the far left. Her head shot up when we walked in, but she stayed seated.

I smiled at her before making my appeal to Officer Rude. "Can we speak alone?"

"You are alone."

"What about him?" I asked, gesturing.

"That's just Randy. He's sleeping it off. He won't even know you're here."

For the first time in my whole life, I wished I were a lawyer. A lawyer could tell Officer Rude that they wanted—and deserved—a private room. They'd get it, too. But since I was no one, just a newcomer who stuck out like a sore thumb in this small town, the officer left without so much as a backward glance.

It would serve her right if I rearranged all the walls in here, I thought bitterly. Just made a big 'ole hole behind Josie and walked the two of us out. Dottie could, apparently, wipe everyone's memory.

Then again, she might haul me off to witches' prison for flashy magic I had no business attempting. I had no desire to find out what it was like there. Or I might set off an explosion like my first attempt at remodeling the mansion.

Once the door clanged into place, Josie stood uncertainly and walked toward the front of the cell. I vowed to come up with an anti-listening spell as soon as I could. For all we knew, Randy was a police officer planted to pick up intel.

"Hey," she said.

"Hey." I nodded toward Randy. "We're not alone, so I don't want you to say anything about what happened."

"I wouldn't even know what to say. I can't believe they arrested me."

"Other than that, how are you?"

"Okay." She tugged at her neckline. "This jumpsuit is itchy."

Silently, I sent a request to the threads to soften, to not irritate Josie's skin. She said nothing, but after a few seconds, she seemed to relax.

Thank you! I said to the threads silently.

Even the fabric felt happier now. Maybe the threads didn't enjoy being all stiff, either. Or maybe they just wanted to be appreciated.

I feel you, threads.

"Can I bring you anything? I've already called a lawyer."

"I know, thanks. He stopped by earlier," she said. "He doesn't think I'm going to get bail."

"Detective Pratt said pretty much the same thing," I told her. "But I'm still going to offer to put up the money."

"No, don't."

"What? Why not?"

"My lawyer said bail isn't common in these types of cases. He thinks the hearing will be just a formality. A quick 'no bail,' and he'll be appointed to represent me. For another, you're new in town. You just opened your business. If word gets out that you're friends with someone accused of murder, no one will touch the place with a ten-foot pole."

I shrugged. "At the moment, the place is a crime scene. I don't have any guests, anyway."

I broke off awkwardly, realizing that they probably had concluded the investigation, since Josie was here and all. Detective Pratt said I could move back in last night. They were moving forward on the assumption that they'd caught the killer. The only way they would admit they were wrong was if I found the correct person and either spelled them into admitting it or located some firm evidence.

After Grandma Vera died, the only person I could count on was myself. Now Josie was counting on me, too.

Hopefully, I was enough.

"I'm so sorry," she said. "I put you in this position. I should never have applied for that position."

"Listen, I'm going to get you out of here. I'll keep investigating, figure out what really happened."

So will my cat and ghost, I didn't add. You know, assuming the ghost stopped exploring the wonders of the twenty-first century and decided to help. Any minute, he'd be asking me to set up TikTok for him.

"C'mon, Emma. If trained police officers couldn't find the real killer, what makes you think you can do it?"

"Because I have magic."

"Listen, this isn't some mystical treasure hunt. This is *murder*. People get killed trying to track down killers. If anything happened to you, I'd never forgive myself."

"I appreciate your concern, but I can't leave you here."

She looked around. "Honestly? This is better than what my husband would do if he found me. Let it go. I'll be okay."

My heart lurched at the words because I recognized what she was really saying. After being let down by so many people who were supposed to care about her, Josie was afraid to believe I would help her. It broke my heart.

At the same time, giving her false hope wouldn't help. I didn't know that I *could* save her, and I didn't want to make any promise I couldn't keep. Something also told me not to mention what Detective Pratt had told me. If she got her hopes up and her husband didn't go to jail, she would feel worse.

Instead of arguing, I asked if there was anything I could bring her before heading back out.

I marched straight to Detective Pratt's desk, which would have been much more intimidating if I hadn't had to stand there and wait for him to get off a call. He pointedly ignored me for long enough that I started to wonder if he was actually listening to someone or just pretending.

Finally, Detective Pratt hung up his phone and turned to me. "How can I help you, Emma?"

"Listen. Josie didn't kill Martha."

"I understand she's your friend—"

"Tuesday morning, when Josie went into the kitchen, Martha thought she was trying to steal her cinnamon roll recipe. Josie had no reason to want that recipe. It doesn't make sense. But then I talked to Lydia at the farmer's market, and she's been trying to convince Martha to sell it to her for months. She's also got scratches on her hands and no alibi. Please, just talk to her."

"That's the other woman you said argued with Martha on Tuesday morning?"

"One of them. Martha was apparently having a bad day, because she also snapped at her daughter-in-law. I think it's worth looking at both of them. Maybe they were working together."

"It wasn't Darlene."

"How can you be so sure?"

"She works at the General Store every morning. Shipments come in on Monday night, so Tuesday is their busiest morning. At least a dozen people saw her there. I already asked." He smiled at me. "Believe it or not, we *have* been investigating this. I don't arrest people willy-nilly."

I visibly deflated at that. "I'm sorry. I just want to help."

"I know, and I appreciate it. You're a good friend. But I have to ask you to let the police force handle this. We're trained investigators, and we know everyone in town. You can't just move in and start throwing around accusations. Someone might take it the wrong way."

"Is that a threat?"

"Not from me. I want you to be careful. It would be a

shame if you got hurt so soon after becoming an heiress. Take some time to live a little."

"I've been taking care of myself a long time, Detective."

"Then maybe it's time to let someone else help you out. I'm giving you friendly advice. Leave this to the professionals. That's not a request."

So that's how he wanted to play it. Then it wasn't worth continuing this conversation. I wasn't going to rest until I found Martha's killer, and if Detective Pratt refused to help, I had no use for him. No one believed I could do this. A month ago, I might have agreed with them. A lifetime of failed relationships and job experiences had set me up to doubt my abilities. But I was a new person.

New magic, new job, new friends, new life.

"I know, I know. Stay out of it or you'll arrest me. You're starting to sound like a broken record."

Spinning around, I stormed out. I would find out who killed Martha to save Josie. I didn't have so many friends I could afford to give one of them up without a fight.

TWENTY

Since Josie asked me not to attend the arraignment, I begrudgingly took a taxi home from the police station. Ditching my ride hadn't been my smartest idea. At least sitting in the back seat while a stranger drove gave me time to think.

Once I arrived, I went into the kitchen and stood inside the door, glaring at the room. This was my first time alone here since finding Martha. She was gone, of course, as was her spirit. Nothing of her should have lingered in the air, and I didn't get any sense of her presence. Yet the room still felt different. Maybe it wanted me to recall its memories. Or maybe I was different.

Only three chairs stood at the table. The police took the chair where Martha was killed as evidence. I hated the vacant space, just sitting there as a visual reminder. The whole set needed to be replaced as soon as I'd found the killer.

There had to be some way to figure this out, whether with magic or logic. On the fridge was a notepad intended for shopping lists. I grabbed it before rummaging in the junk drawer by the dishwasher for a working pen. Sometimes writing things down helped me organize my thoughts when nothing else worked.

What did I know? Martha had been at the wooden table when she died, rolling out dough to make cinnamon rolls. The police had taken samples of everything, although I didn't know what they hoped to find in a tablespoon of filling. Martha hadn't been poisoned.

Detective Pratt thought the killer had come in from the back door. That made sense. My row of apron hooks still hung there, now missing the murder weapon and the one Martha had been wearing when she died. The killer could have opened the door, grabbed the apron, and approached Martha from behind. She'd been blasting the radio, which could explain why she hadn't heard anything. But who was it? And why?

Argh!

Frustrated, I kicked at the tile floor. Ouch.

A knock at the outside door made me look up. To my surprise, Cliff stood on the other side. I opened the door with a furrowed brow. "Hey. I'm sorry, were you supposed to be working today?"

"No, I saw the police cars on my way home last night, and I thought you could use a friend," he said. "Is everything okay?"

"Not even a little bit. I barely know where to start."

He lifted his arms, revealing two plastic bags I hadn't even noticed. "I brought Chinese food if you want to unload."

I'd barely even thought about eating since we got home from the game last night. I'd been so wrapped up in my thoughts and how to help Josie. But now, as the familiar scent of chicken fried rice hit my nose, my stomach growled.

"Listen, I'm sorry about my dad. Our house belonged to my grandparents, and it's all he's ever known. For a long time, we kept it up as a working farm. That farmers market back there? We started that."

"Really? I had no idea."

"Yeah. A few years ago, his doctors said he needed to take things slower. I help where I can, but I'm no farmer. So we came up with the idea of starting a B&B. It brings in enough to pay the property taxes, but when someone younger moved to town, he got nervous."

How nervous? Nervous enough to kill Martha and shut me down? Toby was pretty tall. If he'd slipped in behind her while she was working at the table, all he had to do was wrap it around her neck.

I glanced toward the door uneasily and sipped my water. "Is that why he sent you over? To spy on me?"

Cliff snorted. "Dad might be ornery, but he's not stupid. He saw you spending so much money to remodel and figured you might as well direct some our way."

It was too bad Toby had taken such an antagonistic approach. If I knew he needed help, I would have just given it to him. But paying Cliff to do the work felt less like charity, so maybe it felt more palatable to them. Plus, the more work I found, the more often I could see him.

"How's the bathroom coming?" I asked.

"Good! I ordered the low-flow toilet you wanted. The nearby stores didn't have it. Should be in next Tuesday. Meanwhile, I'll work on the sink and the light fixtures. Did you say you want to finish the basement?"

"I've been thinking about it, but shouldn't we focus on one thing at a time?"

"Definitely. I just figured I could give you an estimate while we wait. I could go down, do some measurements, have a reason to see you again..."

A warm flush crept up my cheeks. "You don't need a reason. But I'll happily give you a tour of the grounds. It's beautiful this time of year."

"I'm sure it is," he said.

He held out his hand. I took it. Together, we headed outside. It had been so long since I had any romance in my life. Cliff was so sweet. With all that had been going on the past few days, maybe this was exactly what I needed.

AFTER CLIFF LEFT, I DECIDED TO MOVE BACK INTO THE MANSION. I was frustrated with the police and annoyed that I couldn't figure out what had happened to Martha. My nervous energy needed to go somewhere, and carrying my stuff up two flights of stairs could help. It might have sounded foolish to voluntarily sleep in a place where someone had been murdered, but in the mansion, I had magical protection spells placed by a stronger witch than me, plus a ghost to warn me if anyone came too close.

Back in the cottage, I dragged my duffle bags out from under the bed and put them on top. I unzipped each, pulling the opening as wide as possible. Then I reached for my magic. Tugging on that now-familiar thread, I pulled all of my clothes toward me. Something responded, but nothing happened.

A series of small thuds made my hair stand on end. Someone might be trying to get in!

Then I realized the problem. My clothes had come toward me as requested. Each article ran into the front of the drawers. Thread magic didn't include the ability to manipulate small wooden objects. At least, not yet. After opening each drawer and the closet door, I tried again.

First, my undergarments floated out of the top drawer like a magician pulling handkerchiefs from his sleeves. Fear of messing this up made it impossible to breathe. But slowly, inch by inch, I moved all of the bras and panties I'd brought with me into the bag.

The process took forever, but with practice, this spell could theoretically be performed in a few seconds. Next were my shorts, socks, then shirts. Finally, the few items hanging in my closet. I zipped each bag and took a deep breath before hefting them onto my shoulders. Although I didn't expect anyone to be around, Dottie's warning rang in my head. *No magic where civilians could see.* What if someone dropped by?

Outside, as expected, the property was vacant. Not even Pink was in sight. It would be nice to have a way to summon that cat, but for now, I was on my own.

At the base of the curving staircase in the foyer, I dropped the bags and sent my magic to the threads holding each one together. Mentally, I urged them upwards. To my shock, the bags rose steadily.

This was so awesome.

Following my direction, the bags moved up the staircase, around the second floor landing, and up toward my room. Once we were entirely out of sight of the main floor, I allowed myself to push a little faster. By the time I dropped the bags on my rug and collapsed onto the bed, I felt both tired and exhilarated. Knowing about the magic had nothing on actually feeling it flow through my veins. Even with all the minor spells I'd performed, this was the first major working since that fateful first day here.

It took a few minutes to catch my breath, but having stretched my magical wings, it was time to tackle a new project: finding out what happened to Martha. There had to be a spell to help me, whether in this house or hidden in the depths of the internet. Eventually, I'd find it.

Up in my room, it took less than a minute to put my clothes away. Amazing.

Then I flipped through Walter's spell book, hoping to find anything useful before storing it back in the trunk. Still nothing. With a sigh of exasperation, I dropped it and fell back onto the rug. The book thudded to the bottom with an echo.

An echo? The trunk's frame should be solid. Hold on. Rolling over, I examined the wood near the floor. Then I pulled myself up and peered into the opening. With one arm, I leaned down to touch the bottom of the trunk. With the other, I stretched to the floor.

Yup.

My left arm definitely reached at least a couple of inches further than my right. Either the floor here had a drastic tilt, or the trunk had a false bottom. Curious, I knocked.

The sound echoed back.

Definitely hollow.

I shot upright so fast, I nearly smacked my face on the lid. Pink and Walter had been holding out on me! After pulling everything out of the trunk, I pressed the bottom, hoping to unlock a hidden catch. When my initial probes didn't work, I began at the far right corner and pressed every inch, looking for the release.

Five frustratingly long minutes later, I sat back on my heels. How did I open this thing?

"Grandpa!" I yelled. That should bring him running. Sure enough, a moment later, he popped into the space beside me.

"I asked you not to—what are you doing?"

"How do I open this thing?"

"If I let you in, it wouldn't be much of a hiding place, now would it?"

I sighed. "Will you at least tell me what's in there? It's important."

"Nope. That's my trunk."

Pink pushed open the bedroom door and trotted over to me. "It's exactly what you think."

"Hey! Whose side are you on?" Walter asked.

"She feeds me," Pink replied. "You don't even scratch my ears anymore."

"I don't have solid hands!"

"How do I access the secret compartment?" I asked.

Walter's face turned stony. "What secret compartment?"

"I hope you didn't play poker much in life," I said. "You'd have lost your shirt."

"Insulting me isn't the way to get help."

"No? Maybe I should reach out to an old friend for you, get back some other thing you loaned them thirty years ago. Come on. You owe me."

Pink meowed at him.

"Hey!" I said. "It's rude to talk about someone right in front of them when they can't understand."

Walter made a face at me. "You don't get to hear everything. In this case, though, I might as well tell you. He said you're ready."

"Ready? For what?"

"For the spell book hidden in the secret compartment, of course," Pink said. "You can't open it because it's protected with magic."

Walter must have been a very strong witch for his protection spells to last so long after his death. Maybe the house lent him extra power because that's where he specialized.

"How do I open it?"

Pink started to say something, but Walter interrupted. "Not so fast. If she's really ready, let her figure it out."

This was absolutely not the time for a "teach a woman to fish" moment, but I sensed that pushing wouldn't help. Instead, I closed my eyes, took a deep breath, and counted to ten. Using a thread of magic, I probed the trunk, feeling for any clues. There, near the back left corner. The false bottom was sewn into place with tiny stitches that would be imperceptible to most people. I coaxed the thread toward me. Nothing happened.

Maybe this was not the time to be polite. With my magic, I yanked at the threads, demanding them to release themselves from the velvety material covering the wooden bottom. Tiny bits of silk flew out of the trunk, peppering the room around me. Several hit me in the face. One landed on Pink's head. He shook several times and sneezed to dislodge it. Three more went right through Walter, much to his chagrin.

"See? I knew you could do it," Pink said. "Although next time, try a little finesse."

"Finesse wasn't working," I muttered as I reached inside to lift the false bottom out of the trunk. Underneath was a thin leather-bound volume with yellowed pages, older than the other books I'd inherited. Slowly, almost reverently, I opened the cover and read the first page. "Property of Evelyn Sparrow."

"My grandmother," Walter said. "She'd be pretty impressed you found that."

"To be honest, I'm rather impressed with myself right now," I replied. "Was she a hearth witch, too?"

"No, that came from my father's lineage. Grandma Evelyn specialized in memory magic."

"She could do memory wipes?"

"Cool your jets," Pink said. "Those spells are very delicate. Try them before you're ready, and the entire Witches' Council will knock down your door when you mess it up."

"Thanks for the vote of confidence."

"There is a pretty cool spell in there she made for my father, though. Combines memory magic with thread magic. For when you're ready." Walter looked so proud. Whether of me or his grandmother, I couldn't say.

The spell on the first page was written in an unfamiliar language. I pulled out my phone to take a picture so I could upload it to Google Translate, but Pink stopped me.

"That's not a human language," he said. "It's written in a magical code. The words will reveal themselves when the time is right."

Of course. Patience had never been my strong suit, but I tried not to show how annoying this was. At least I had magic.

Then I turned another page and my breath caught at the words. "A Peek into the Past."

"Will this spell show me what happened to Martha?"

"That was one of my mother's favorite spells when I was a kid," Walter said. "She always knew who snuck cookies out of the jar. Took me years to figure out how she did it."

"The crumbs on your clothes gave quite a hint," Pink said. "Not everything requires magic."

The two of them bickered like an old married couple. Sometimes it was charming, but right now, Pink's words jumped out at me. "You knew Walter as a child?"

"Of course."

"How old *are* you?" I asked.

He sniffed. "That is none of your concern."

"Nice try," Walter said. "Not even I know that."

Turning back to the spell, I skimmed the page, taking in the words. The incantation seemed pretty straightforward. Closing my eyes, I took a deep breath.

"Not here," Walter said. "You'd only get a memory of what happened in your bedroom at the time of Martha's death. You need to be where she was to relive her experience."

Right. I should've known. Hugging the book to my chest, I scrambled to my feet. I didn't even stop to put the trunk back together, just raced down the stairs and through the kitchen door.

Although common sense told me not to be silly, before starting I flipped the deadbolt on the door leading outside. Better to be safe. It took many deep breaths before I felt capable of moving around the room.

Hardly daring to breathe, I pulled the curtains shut and turned off the lights. Then I placed candles on the table and placed a stick of incense in a holder in the middle. According to the spell book, the magic would be strongest at the spot where the event to be recalled occurred—in this case, the kitchen table. The three chairs remaining looked exactly like the one where Martha had taken her last breath. Rather than choosing one to sit, I moved into the open space. Part of me hesitated to fill this space, despite knowing the dining set held no malevolent energy. Martha had left this plane, the killer was long gone, and the table was just a table.

The book went into the middle, opened to the spell. While reading a verse aloud, I lit each candle and the incense. I placed my hands on the open book and closed my eyes, focusing on my memories of Martha. Then I opened my eyes and read the rest of the incantation aloud.

As I spoke, the room got hazy. Everything spun around me as time rewound to Tuesday morning. When it stopped, a thick dough lay flat on the table with a layer of butter on top. A brownish substance that must have been cinnamon and sugar covered about a third of the dough. I tried to turn my head, but I couldn't. This must be Martha's memory of the moment she died. I was only an observer in this scene, not an active participant.

All of a sudden, pink flashed before my eyes. The apron. It settled around my neck. I choked. Martha choked. I had to remind myself that it wasn't real. Intense pressure on my neck made me gasp. Hands came up, scrambling to remove the apron, get some air, harm the person behind her.

A hiss of pain told me she'd struck a soft spot with her nails. *Come on, Martha. See something.*

There was nothing to see. The spell showed me Martha's final moments exactly as she had lived them, and she hadn't seen a thing. As she toppled onto the table, I strained, desperate to see or hear anything. All I heard was footsteps across the floor, and the kitchen door opening. My gaze landed on the clock, which gave me Martha's time of death at nine thirty-seven.

Whoever killed Martha must have left only a few minutes before I entered. I shuddered to realize how close

I'd come to being a second victim. What if I'd walked faster through the woods instead of enjoying the view?

My first instinct was to do the spell again but I was very new at this. Recalling the past had wiped me out. My eyelids weighed a thousand pounds each. As badly as I wanted to try another spell, it was impossible. My limbs felt like butter. The stairs weren't even manageable in this state, and my magic burned at its lowest level since before the curse ended.

Mustering every bit of remaining energy, I stumbled through the swinging door into the living room and collapsed onto the couch.

Tomorrow, I would start over.

CHAPTER
TWENTY-ONE

When I woke up the next morning, I felt much better physically and worse emotionally. The problem with going back to the witching board was that I'd run out of ideas. With a groan, I dragged myself into the kitchen. I hadn't eaten since early yesterday, and food would restore me better than anything.

Inside the kitchen, I found Walter waiting for me. He sat on the counter beside the coffee maker, staring at it forlornly.

"I miss coffee."

"Would it help if I poured you a cup?"

He shook his head. "Somehow, I don't think so. Now, how do we find this killer?"

"It's possible that magic isn't the answer."

"You gave it a good shot. Let's talk it out."

Before sitting at the table, I started the coffeemaker. Inside the pantry, I found the muffins I bought the day Martha got killed. I wasn't entirely sure how they'd gotten there, but maybe one of the police officers had picked them up. They were a little dented from where they'd hit the ground, but still vastly superior to any food I might try to cook. It felt weird not to offer one to Walter, so I did.

He chuckled. "That would be something, wouldn't it? I used to love a good blueberry muffin."

Pulling out a chair facing the kitchen door, I sat at the table. "I don't believe Josie would hurt anyone. I wish we knew what evidence they had. Can you sneak into the police station, look around?"

"Sure, but I can't touch anything. Unless the information we need is sitting out, I'm no help," Walter said. "The best way to prove Josie's innocence is to find the guilty party. Let's talk this out. Why would someone kill Martha?"

"On TV, it's always the husband. That's not helpful, though. Her husband died when I was in college," I said.

"Twenty years ago. She was very emotional when she saw him again, but it's possible she had started dating since then."

I shook my head. The look on her face when that door opened and her husband waited on the other side told me everything I needed to know: she'd never moved on from his death. "No. She was still in love with him. She wore her wedding rings after all this time. But there could have been someone who *wanted* to date her. A spurned lover?"

"Now we're talking!"

"I'll see if I can find a way to ask her kids about that possibility. I could always call Darlene, ask if she found the recipe after we spoke. That might give me an opening."

"What about the kids? Could they have killed her?"

I thought about it. "It sounded like, when they allowed her to move in, her son thought she was going to be at his beck and call anytime he needed a babysitter. If she was helping out, I don't see him giving that up so easily. Then again, that was why she applied for the job here. She said she wanted to be out and about, prove that she had other contributions to the household. Maybe he got mad that she wouldn't be available all the time." I shook my head. "If you ask me, the daughter-in-law is a better suspect. Darlene swore Martha hated her, and there was weirdness around Martha's refusal to share her recipes."

"What about you?" he asked.

That gave me pause. "What about me? You can't think I killed her."

"Are you sure you didn't see or hear anything important? You found her. Where were you before that?"

"At the farmers market," I said. "I was talking to Beth. She mentioned that Martha had been in earlier and told them she was working for me. Then Martha insulted her sister. They argued, and both of them walked away to cool off."

"That's very interesting."

"Definitely. When I went back Wednesday morning, Lydia admitted that they didn't get along, but she didn't mention the argument. She wanted Martha's recipe for cinnamon rolls, and Martha wasn't giving anything away. Apparently, they're pretty darn good. Everyone wants to know what's in them."

Walter snorted. "Cinnamon, butter, sugar. Lots of all three. That's how Mom made them."

"Touché. But wait—I was going somewhere with that. Lydia had bandages on her hands."

"How did she get injured?"

"Good question. I didn't manage to slip it into the conversation. When I performed the spell to see how Martha died, she definitely scratched her attacker. That could explain the injury. Lydia was upset with Martha, and she doesn't have an alibi." I drained my coffee cup and stood up. "Maybe we should take a walk and find out what her story is."

"It could be dangerous to confront a killer, you know. I would be derelict in my duty as your grandfather if I let you put yourself in harm's way."

"I'm not going to confront her. Just have a friendly, neighborly chat. I promise, if I find anything I'll call the police. Detective Pratt already warned me about interfering."

"Good. I knew I liked him."

I locked up, and we took off for the path through the forest. We'd barely entered the clearing where the farmers market was located before someone called my name. Then we spotted Lydia waving from her booth.

"Who's that?" Walter asked.

"That's our primary suspect," I said as I waved back.

She beckoned.

Walter asked, "That's Lydia? And Beth? The last time I saw them, they were barely out of diapers. How can they be grown up and running a food stand?"

"Same way as me. It's been almost thirty years."

He sighed. "Being dead, you sure miss a lot."

"Help me solve this, and I'll take you out any time you want," I said, heading for the stall to say hello. "I already got you theater tickets."

"Ask about the bandages," Walter hissed.

Right. Time for sleuthing.

I pasted a broad smile on my face. "Good morning, Lydia."

"Emma! You're becoming a real regular. How are you?"

"Well, turns out, I have more of a sweet tooth than I thought. I can't stay away. Your baked goods are amazing."

Then, as if noticing for the first time, I said, "What happened to your hands?"

"Oh, it was the stupidest thing. I was out in the woods, trekking along, when I spotted these blackberry bushes. I got all excited, thinking about how I would use them to make fresh tarts, maybe topped with some vanilla-scented cream. Martha can keep her cinnamon rolls; these were going to be perfection. They would have given her a real run for her money at the county fair this year." She sighed. "Well, in theory. Unfortunately, I'm not much of an outdoors person. When I reached for the berries, I lost my balance, grabbed the vine to catch myself, and got a palm full of thorns."

"Ouch! That sounds terrible." I wasn't sure whether to believe her, but I put as much sincerity as I could muster into the words.

"Yeah. Thus ends my career as a forager. Apparently, farmers can breed them without thorns. I'll find a stand next time. Not that it matters anymore." She shook her head. "That reminds me. Emma, I owe you a thank you."

"Me? What did I do?"

"You gave Darlene the recipe for Martha's cinnamon rolls. I don't know how you convinced that old bat to share where she'd hidden it, but you must be some kind of gift from the heavens. Darlene sold it to me yesterday afternoon and now..." She pulled a small bakery box out from under the shelf and put it on the counter with great fanfare. "Ta-da! My gift to you. As of today, my cookbook is complete."

My spidey senses were off the charts. Something was very, very wrong about all this.

At the moment, you couldn't pay me a million dollars to eat something Lydia baked specially for me. The look

Walter gave me suggested the same. "That's so sweet! You shouldn't have!"

"Oh, it was nothing. I needed to test the recipe, anyway —I wouldn't put it past Martha to leave out a key ingredient or something. Bad enough she didn't have half the amounts. I had to figure it out like a contestant on the *The Great British Baking Show*. Spent all of last night working on the proportions." She smiled broadly. "But it's okay, because her shenanigans got me twenty-five percent off Darlene's price. Once I get these cookbooks going, we'll make a killing."

The words sent a chill down my spine. Martha refused to share her recipe, and now Lydia got it from Darlene, who never liked her mother-in-law. Given the amount of time Martha said her rolls needed to rise, Darlene must have called her as soon as she got home from the funeral. Had Lydia known Darlene would sell the recipe? Had Darlene been aware she had a buyer waiting in the wings, prepared to hand over cash as soon as she got Martha out of the way? How did they even know each other?

If Lydia killed Martha, maybe she took the weddings rings to return them to Darlene. Or Darlene could have taken them as a family heirloom. Either of them could have dropped the rings by mistake while climbing through the pool house window.

The plot was thickening, fast. If only Walter and I could sort it out, we'd have Josie home in no time.

"You'll have to let me know when the books are available," I said. "I'd love to buy one."

Walter snorted. "Just promise you won't make any of the recipes. I don't want to haunt a burnt-out shell."

With great effort, I ignored him.

"I'll do one better," Lydia said. "You'll get the first one

off the press, signed and gift-wrapped. Really, I can't thank you enough."

Despite my protests, she forced the box of cinnamon rolls into my hands before we left. As soon as we got out of earshot, Walter said, "Normally when someone dies, the other members of the community are less thrilled about it."

"Yes," I said, my mind still mulling the possibilities. "Barely contained glee at the death of a long-time acquaintance is not a good look."

"You think she had something to do with it?"

Looking down at the baked goods in my hands, I wished I knew a spell to detect poison. But that was ridiculous. I'd been watching too many reruns of *Murder, She Wrote*. Even if Lydia killed Martha, she had no reason to think I was on to her. It wouldn't make sense for her to poison me. Still, I made a mental note to ask Josie if she knew a spell you could put on food to test it for poison.

Besides, Lydia wasn't the only one who profited here. After hearing how quickly Darlene sold her family's prized secret recipe, I suddenly felt the urge to have another talk with the woman.

CHAPTER
TWENTY-TWO

J ust because Detective Pratt refused to consider Darlene's possible involvement in Martha's death didn't mean I couldn't confront her. She'd sold that recipe practically before her mother-in-law was in the ground. Maybe she and Lydia concocted the entire scheme together. Working at the General Store gave Darlene a great alibi. Everyone knew her and people saw her there when the store was busy. Did she use the rest of the town to get away with murder?

Walter clapped with delight when I invited him to come along. "You're going to confront a murderer? Oh, yes! Come on, Nancy Drew!"

"Nancy's sidekick wasn't a ghost."

"Then call me Bess. Let's go. I can't wait to see you show them all how you figured it out, resulting in a dramatic confession."

"We're also not on *Murder, She Wrote*."

Walter sighed heavily. "A shame. Do you think you can find old episodes of that?"

"I can find old episodes of just about anything you want as soon as we stop Darlene."

"What are you waiting for, Slowpoke? Let's go!"

Turned out, the thing I waited for was a working mode of transportation. My car battery shockingly hadn't charged itself overnight, and it would take forever to walk to town. Luckily, there was still that bike in the barn. Whose bike? Not a clue, but the tires were full of air and all the parts looked like they were in the right place. Presumably, anything in the barn belonged to me, although the lack of dirt and cobwebs made me wonder how long this had been sitting there. Maybe the police had cleaned it off for some reason. Or Josie?

If she'd had a bike in her trunk, she wouldn't mind me using it under the circumstances. I made a note to ask her once she was free.

Before I pushed off, Walter climbed onto the seat behind me. He couldn't sit, but he hovered. Then he stuck his feet out on either side of me, threw his head back, and cheered. His enthusiasm made me smile.

Soon enough, I pedaled into the parking lot of the Willow Falls General Store. Outside, it looked like a log cabin. The whole thing brought up memories of the old shops I'd seen on shows like *Anne of Green Gables* when I was a kid.

The inside was every bit as cozy. Row after row of wooden shelves and the smell of freshly baked cookies in the air. Like any grocery story, they sold food, including a small produce section—most of which claimed to be locally grown. They offered pies and cookies baked on the premises. But you could also get cleaning supplies, books, crayons, needle and thread, and all kinds of other things. It was like the world's smallest Target.

"Can I help you?" a voice beside me asked.

Turning, I spotted not Darlene but someone about twenty years older. Medium height, medium build, with a pointed nose, sharp chin, and overly bleached blonde hair. She looked vaguely familiar, and I realized she'd been at Martha's funeral. Other side of the room, near the middle. Not close enough to be family.

"I'm Emma," I said. "I was looking for Darlene. Is she working this morning?"

"You didn't hear?" The woman leaned forward as if she was about to impart the juiciest bit of gossip.

Hoping to encourage her, I leaned in. "No! What happened?"

"Darlene quit! She had yesterday off for the funeral— the whole store was closed so we could all go. Then last night, she called and told me she didn't need my job anymore. Apparently, her mother-in-law's life insurance was enough to let her stay home with the kids until they start school. Can you imagine?"

I could imagine, actually, given my own circumstances. But was the life insurance story true? How much did Lydia pay for that recipe? What was in those baked goods to make them worth the kind of money that let a person quit their job?

With effort, I reined myself back. It was possible that Darlene had told the truth, and Martha had procured a large insurance policy. Getting the money for selling the recipe might have just been icing on the... er, cinnamon rolls.

"Wow," I said, completely at a loss for words. "Do you know if she was at work on Tuesday morning?"

"Yeah, definitely. Darlene worked every Tuesday. Now I

need a replacement. You aren't looking for a job, are you? I can give you full-time."

"No, I run a bed-and-breakfast on the edge of town. Martha was my chef." I paused. "I'm sorry. I never got your name."

"Sadie. My family's owned this store for decades. Darlene is my cousin, which is the main reason we let her work here as long as she did." She lowered her voice to a stage whisper. "Between you and me, she wasn't the best cashier."

"Your secret's safe with me," I said. "Did you actually see her working on Tuesday morning? Could she have left and come back?"

"I guess she could have, but she didn't. We were slammed all morning. She was either in the back unpacking boxes or up front helping me bag to keep the line down."

"Does she get a lunch break?"

"Sure. New York requires an unpaid lunch break of at least a half hour. I'm not messing with that, not as a small business owner. You tell them that if anyone asks."

"Would you know if she left?" I asked, trying to keep the discussion on track.

Sadie shrugged. "Depends on whether I was paying attention. Why does it matter? What's with the interest in Darlene?"

Now I was treading on thin ice. There was no good reason for me to be so interested in where Darlene was when her mother-in-law died. I couldn't say I wanted to verify her alibi. Since the whole point of coming was to question Darlene about selling the recipe, I should go.

"No reason," I said. "Just wondering if she ever went to the farmers market for lunch."

"Sometimes, I guess. Her best friend works there. But

there wouldn't have been any reason to do that, because Lydia dropped in on Tuesday morning."

That stopped me in my tracks. If Darlene and Lydia were together before Martha died, maybe my theory wasn't so far-fetched. "You're sure?"

"Positive. She looked annoyed. Still wearing her apron, complaining about blackberries."

The scratches. My heart jumped into my throat. "Do you have any idea what time that would have been?"

"Yeah, sure," she said. "I pulled the security tapes for the police the other day, so we checked the time. Lydia arrived around nine-thirty and left about ten minutes later. They were together in the back, the whole time."

This conversation completely deflated me. If Lydia and Darlene were here together at the time of Martha's murder, it couldn't have been either of them. There was no way for either of them to have gotten to the mansion, killed Martha, and disappeared before I'd gotten back. Beth was talking to me so she couldn't have been involved, either.

My suspects were dropping like a poorly made soufflé.

Trying not to show my disappointment, I thanked Sadie for the information and turned to leave.

Toward the front of the store, I stopped. Since I was here anyway, I might as well do something useful. The job posting that fired Toby up so much on Monday was still hanging on the board. It felt like a million years since I'd tacked it up there. While I was here, I should take it down.

The message board looked the same as when I'd hung my notices: one about the need for a cook, and another announcing that we were open for business. Only a couple of tags had been taken from the cook posting, which wasn't a big surprise. Even though I theoretically would need a new cook if Josie were convicted or if her cooking magic didn't return, leaving it there felt wrong. Reaching up, I unpinned the notice and stuffed it into my pocket.

Another woman paused beside me, scanning the announcements. "Anything good happening around here? I'd love to see some live music or a show."

"The nearest shows I'm aware of are down in Saratoga," I said. "About twenty minutes away. But people post stuff here all the time. Something might come up if you check back."

She continued skimming the pages. "What about local hot spots? Where would you take a guest?"

"I think this bulletin board *is* the local hot spot," I joked. Then, because it could be hard for new residents in a small town to make friends, I said, "By the way, I'm Emma."

"Jane. Have you lived here long?"

I shook my head. "Only a few weeks. Bar Naan has the best Indian food you'll ever taste, but beyond that, I don't know a lot about the local attractions yet."

Another voice chimed in. "Are you looking for a place to stay? A new bed-and-breakfast just opened."

With a smile, I turned toward the interloper. Sadie had apparently decided to insert herself into our conversation, more or less confirming what I thought about her interest in gossip.

"Oh no!" Jane shuddered in response to the inquiry. I was about to get offended when she leaned toward me and lowered her voice. "That place is haunted. A woman DIED there."

"The ghost isn't the woman who died," I said without thinking. "Martha's gone."

The way Jane looked at me said that if I wanted to be a witch with a haunted B&B, I needed to learn to censor myself better. Too many years of being on my own.

After a minute, Sadie laughed. "Funny. They told me the woman who runs the place is funny."

Jane gasped. "It's you! You own the B&B where someone was murdered?"

"I run a local bed-and-breakfast. I'm sorry to say that tragedy occurred there earlier this week, but the police believe it was an isolated occurrence. The place is perfectly safe, and we're back in business as of today." Guess I had a date for reopening, after all. Turning back to Sadie, I said, "Who were you talking to about me? Why would someone tell you I'm funny?"

"It's nothing personal, dear. We talk about everyone around here. When you work in a busy store in a small town like this, you gain information. It's only appropriate to share with interested parties."

Mentally, I sighed. So much for hoping to make a new friend here. Sadie liked stirring the pot and seeing what rose to the surface. Maybe I'd do my shopping in Shady Grove from now on. Or at the big supermarket on the other side of town.

"Martha's death was a tragedy. An evil act done by someone with an axe to grind," I said. "Detective Pratt said there is no reason to think anyone else would be in danger."

"That's true! I hear they have a suspect in custody," Sadie said.

Oh, no. Gossiping about Josie was the last thing I wanted. Hoping to steer the conversation back in the right direction, I said, "I saw you at the funeral."

"I wanted to show my respect. We've known each other for years. Martha was practically family."

Jane was still standing there, looking both fascinated and uncomfortable by our discussion.

I felt exactly the same way. I asked her, "How did you know Martha?"

"I didn't," she said.

"Then who told you someone died at my bed-and-breakfast?"

"The guy who runs the local inn. I was looking at the message board here yesterday morning to find a room. He came over and told me that Emma's bed-and-breakfast wasn't safe. My husband and I booked his place instead."

"You drove to Willow Falls without anywhere to stay?"

"Not exactly. Our car broke down on the way to Montreal. I like staying at B&Bs instead of hotels. You get to know the locals. Learn about the community."

She was learning about the community, alright. Toby was telling people about Martha's murder to book his rooms instead of mine. Toby implied to people there was something off about me. I'd have bet anything he was the one who told Sadie I was "funny," even if she wouldn't admit it. Toby hated me and my business. He claimed I was costing him money and shouldn't be allowed to operate. He threatened to call the city to check my permits.

Toby was such a blusterer; he seemed more comical than threatening. Years of working on the farm helped a person build muscle, though. If he snuck up on Martha while she leaned over the table rolling out dough, it would only take a second to get the apron around her neck. With the advantage of surprise and the leverage of standing over her, he could definitely have done it.

A groan escaped me as I realized how very shortsighted I had been in this investigation. This wasn't about Martha at all. I'd been so focused on Lydia, I'd missed the one person who benefited if my bed-and-breakfast shut down.

CHAPTER
TWENTY-THREE

With my thoughts consuming me, I left the General Store so fast my ghost remained in the dust. He caught up with me as I mounted my borrowed bicycle.

"What's wrong? What happened?" he asked. "Toby's just being Toby."

"Was he 'just being Toby' when he killed Martha?"

If a ghost's face could grow paler, that's what happened. "Really? No. Not Toby."

"I should have seen it sooner," I said as I hit the kick-stand with one foot. "He has the most to gain from someone dying at my bed-and-breakfast."

Before he could reply, I pushed off with an unfortunate wobble that had the effect of sending me right through my grandfather. He shouted indignantly.

"Sorry!" I called back.

If I understood the way this worked, he'd come with me whether or not he "sat" on the bike. Not that I wanted to drag a ghost along behind me.

My mind raced all the way back to the mansion.

Considering how out of shape I was, the trip took much longer than it should have. No matter how many times I rolled the facts over in my head, I reached the same conclusion. Several people had a problem with Martha. Picking a victim with a lot of enemies probably made more sense than coming after me directly—after all, my neighbor was the only person around here with a reason to want me dead. The police would have been knocking on his door in seconds.

It made me sick to realize Toby was so furious with me for opening a competing business, he killed an innocent person to shut me down. But it all made sense. First, he'd threatened me. He'd called the building inspector. He'd spread rumors about me and the house. When none of that worked, he'd made one last futile effort by coming over to warn me on opening day.

After seeing all of those efforts fail, he killed my cook in the kitchen to force me out of business. Toby knew I couldn't cook—he'd dropped by the day I'd made those disgusting cookies. The stench lingered for hours; he'd even commented on it. He definitely saw my ads up at the General Store, so he knew I needed a cook. A bed-and-breakfast without breakfast wouldn't last long.

A bed-and-breakfast where people died would close even faster.

I screeched to a halt at the top of my driveway, wondering what to do now. Storming over there alone and accusing Toby of being a murderer seemed like a great way to get myself killed.

"What about the wedding rings?" Walter asked as soon as we stopped. "Toby didn't have a reason to steal them, did he?"

I shook my head. "Not that I know of, but he didn't keep

them as a trophy. He dropped them. If he needed money, it's possible he took them to sell before realizing they weren't worth a lot. Or maybe he wanted me to think Martha's daughter-in-law killed her and took them. Anything to throw the police off the track. Like how he told people he saw Josie outside the crime scene."

"Seems a little suspicious, doesn't it? Going around accusing everyone you can think of?"

My cheeks grew warm at the thought of how I'd nearly become guilty of the same thing. Suspecting first Lydia, then Darlene. "It almost worked."

Unfortunately, I didn't have enough to get Detective Pratt to make an arrest. Especially not after I told him Darlene was the killer. He'd think I was accusing anyone I could think of to save Josie. If I wanted him to take me seriously, I needed hard evidence.

Toby would never admit what he'd done to me. Maybe he'd confess to his son? If Cliff could get Toby to believe he supported him, that he'd done the right thing, maybe I could get a confession. Then we'd just need Toby to believe we were on his side long enough for the Willow Falls police to show up and arrest him.

Was it legal to record someone in New York without telling them? According to my phone it was, as long as I was a party to the conversation. Maybe Cliff and I could confront Toby together.

Now to figure out how to tell Cliff his father was a murderer and I needed his help to catch him. Wait. I couldn't do that. Not that I intended to let Toby get away with murder just because I had a thing for Cliff, but playing son against father? That wasn't fair. Sure, we barely knew each other, but I didn't want to break his heart. There had to be a better way.

Maybe I could gather more information without revealing why I was there. First things first—were there brambles on the forest path between our houses? Leaving the bike behind, I set off through the woods. Taking a deep breath, I counted to fifty to settle myself and then headed out, hoping to look like someone taking a nature stroll and not an amateur sleuth in way over her head.

Walter moved behind me, remaining uncharacteristically silent. Probably trying to think of a way to talk me out of this, but my mind was made up.

Most of the plants on the path were unfamiliar. I took it all in, moving at a snail's pace to ensure I didn't miss anything. Finally, I spotted what I was looking for. A brown bush lined the path. A few tendrils draped across the dirt where they could be stepped on by unsuspecting passersby. Someone running on the path might pick up a vine and trail it behind them without noticing.

I would expect a person who did the walk all the time to be more careful, but when you had murder on the mind, it might be easy to miss.

The path ahead of me curved. I thought Toby's house was near, but I couldn't be sure. I stopped and turned to Walter. "How far away are we?"

"Nope. Not helping you," he said. "Why don't you go back to the house and look for a map."

"Great idea," I said.

Instead of turning around, I pulled out my phone and opened an app. Thanks to technology, I could orient myself without moving at all.

According to Apple, I was about halfway between the properties. As near as I could tell, there wasn't anything else in this area. No public parking here, because the woods were on my land and Toby's. If anyone had crossed his land to access mine, Toby should have seen them. Yet I hadn't heard even a hint of useful information coming from this direction. Only unfounded rumors pointing to Josie. He must have known the police were looking at her and decided to push them a bit.

With every step, I became more sure Toby had killed Martha. The apron had been taken to a police evidence locker, so I wouldn't find the murder weapon in his house. He needed to admit what he did so Detective Pratt would release Josie.

Before putting my phone back in my pocket, I snapped a picture of the bushes. This path was traveled by enough wildlife that it wasn't easy to pick up any footprints. I'd walked it more than once, and so had both of my neighbors. Footprints weren't the answer, but I felt better being able to say, "Look! My bramble theory wasn't as dumb as you made it sound, Detective."

When I arrived at the house, a sign on the front door told me the bed-and-breakfast was open for business, so I didn't bother knocking. Full of resolve, I opened the front door and strode inside like a woman on a mission.

Toby was nowhere to be seen. The entire front room was empty: no guests, no employees. However, loud voices filtered down the stairwell. I wasn't close enough to hear what they were saying, but they sounded angry. Was a guest in danger? Had someone else come to confront Toby? Maybe Cliff figured it out on his own, and I wouldn't have to be the one to tell him.

"What now?" Walter asked.

"You're a ghost. Explore. Go see who that is and what they're talking about."

"Sounds like they're fighting."

"Make sure no one is injured."

"Fine, fine. I'll be right back. Try not to get yourself in any trouble. Better yet, go back to the mansion and wait for me."

Ignoring his suggestion, I inched toward the stairs, hoping to overhear something good before anyone noticed me. Up one step, stop, listen. Nothing. Another step. Then another. I climbed one at a time, with an aching slowness, but I needed to hear what was being said. Josie's life depended on it. If I made too much noise, they'd stop talking.

Finally, after what seemed a lifetime, I got close enough to make out the words. The people speaking were inside a bedroom at the top of the stairs. Their voice carried through the partially open door. I couldn't see anyone inside, but their conversation came through clearly.

"For me? You can't say you did this for me. I was managing fine. Sure, times are tough, but we've managed tough times before. I'd been thinking about selling some of the land, anyway. It's too much for me." Toby sighed. "Taxes are high, and I'm tired of tending crops."

"But now you don't have to sell! You're the best bed-and-breakfast in the area, and now, you've got an internet presence. This house will be bigger than ever, as soon as Emma leaves."

"I'd rather sell than let an innocent woman die because of me."

"You're so short-sighted. This isn't about Martha. It's about our future."

I knew that voice. Didn't want to. It broke my heart to admit it, but Toby was in there, talking to Martha's killer. It wasn't my neighbor, like I thought.

ADA BELL

It was the guy who'd been flirting with me all week.

To think I'd been taken in by a charming smile and some flirty banter. The whole time I'd been trying to solve the mystery of Martha's killer, he'd been pretending to woo me. Probably wanted to talk me into closing up shop because it was too dangerous or something.

The precarious nature of my situation sank in. Confronting a seventy-five-year-old man hadn't concerned me. Part of me didn't believe he would attack, but at the same time, I could outrun him. Toby was strong from working on the farm, but he was far from fast.

Cliff had said he was away camping with a friend when Martha died. Stupid me, I'd been so smitten by those brown eyes and that charming smile, I hadn't even thought to check his alibi.

My heart wanted to believe that I misunderstood the conversation unfolding in front of me, but really, not much was open to interpretation. I needed to get out of here and call the police as soon as I made sure Toby wasn't in immediate danger.

Bursting in to save him would only get me in trouble. I didn't know if Cliff was armed, but he was well-muscled and at least six inches taller than me. In hand-to-hand combat, I'd be lucky to stomp on his toes without bruising my foot.

Walter was in there, though. If he thought his friend was in danger, he'd tell me. Probably.

"This wasn't what I wanted at all," Toby said loudly, interrupting my thoughts. "I'm an honest business man. I've known Martha my whole life!"

"You've known everyone your whole life. That's why we're in this mess. You didn't want to charge anyone more than they could afford for the fruit and vegetables. You

208

don't ask people to pay a fair rent for the land where they hold the farmers market. You let out rooms below the market rate because you don't want to take advantage of anyone. Meanwhile, they're all taking advantage of you. You could triple all of those numbers and we'd be fine, but you won't."

"My prices are fair," Toby said. "Just because you can gouge people doesn't mean you should. Besides, I can't triple my rates and have any hope of keeping business from going next door. Emma practically gives her rooms away."

"That's why I had to do this. There was no other choice. She's pretty, she's charming, she even has a resident cat! People love cats. If customers start going to her place instead of ours, we can't pay the property taxes. We'll lose the farm."

"Then we lose the farm." Toby's voice was firm. "This is my legacy, boy, not yours. I would never kill someone to maintain the illusion that I'm going to be rich. Money's not worth it. You have to call the police and tell them what you did."

"Don't be ridiculous," Cliff replied. "I saved us. You're not going to turn me in, either. You're going to stay right here. It's a shame you're not feeling well. I'm sure our guests will miss you, but I'll take care of everything."

"What's your plan? Let Josie go to jail for a crime you committed? You going to lock me up in this house so I can't tell the truth? Or are you going to put on a wig and run this place like you're me?"

"I'm not Norman Bates. But I do think you should stay in your room for a few days, think about things. We'll talk when you're feeling better."

"I feel fine!" Toby snapped.

Walter appeared in front of me. "Toby didn't kill

Martha. Cliff is in there, threatening his old man. We need to call the cops. I'm going back to watch them."

Before I could respond, he vanished.

This wasn't good. I needed to get out of here.

Footsteps echoed on the floorboards a few feet away. Not nearly far enough.

Someone was moving toward the door, and I'd bet my life it wasn't Toby. If Cliff opened the bedroom door, he would see me instantly.

Leaning against the wall, I stepped down onto the top step. Then the next. Once I was three steps down and around the bend, I could almost breathe.

The door opened.

My heart pounded.

I needed to move.

Inside the room, Toby said something. Now I was too far away to hear, but grateful that he distracted his son long enough for me to step down again. Every inch brought me closer to escape.

Walter popped up beside me. "He's coming!"

My ghost's obvious distress motivated me to move faster. I took two quick steps. The floorboard squeaked below my feet, bringing me to an immediate halt.

Cliff's voice carried clearly down the stairwell. "What was that? Who's there?"

"Don't stop!" Walter said. "Quick, do a spell!"

A terrific idea, but that huge spell last night really drained me. Could I save myself with magic?

Closing my eyes, I reached for my power. It lay inside me like a wet noodle. When I tried to pick it up, it slid out of my grasp. There wasn't enough magic for even a simple spell.

Cliff's footsteps came closer, and suddenly, there was no time to experiment.

No longer trying to be quiet, I turned and fled down the stairs. Three steps from the front door, someone grabbed the back of my shirt. A sudden impact sent me to my knees. Everything went black.

TWENTY-FOUR

Whenen I woke up, a big patch of brown filled my vision. I blinked a few times to clear it, but nothing changed. Something smelled like dirt. Oh, right. It was dirt. Inches below my face, several feet closer than I wanted dirt to be. What happened?

My head pounded. I tried to reach up to touch the throbbing spot above my left ear, but my arms wouldn't to move. Where was I?

With a rush, it all came back. I'd deduced that Toby killed Martha, gone over to dig for evidence like a fool without telling anyone where I was going, and discovered that it was actually his son Cliff, who I had recently been dreaming about kissing.

Ugh.

Then he whacked me over the head, and now I was lying on the hard, cold ground.

Also, my ghost disappeared. Whether he'd stayed in the bed-and-breakfast after I got knocked out or went back to the mansion, I'd probably never know. Weird he wouldn't have come along when Cliff brought me out here when I still wore the locket. Maybe I had to be awake for the magic to work.

Where had my attacker gone? If he was nearby, I didn't want Cliff to know I'd woken up. Rolling over would alert him, so that was out. At least until I figured out more about my situation. Birds chirped overhead. The area was lit, but not super bright. We were probably in the woods between my house and Toby's, but the actual location could be anywhere. Wonderful. If only I had plant magic, I would ask the brambles to choke him. You know, if he hadn't finished digging my grave by the time my magic returned.

Closing my eyes, I reached for my powers to see what kind of damage could be done. The spool flickered dimly. I reached for the magic. Nothing happened. The energy was still too depleted from yesterday's working. I wanted to kick myself for attempting such a huge spell with so little train-ing. Yes, it worked, and it was important—but now I might die.

The forest was full of dangers. Cliff could chuck me down a hill, I would break my neck, and no one would have any reason to suspect him. They'd all seen us together at the farmers market. He could even say we'd gone for a hiking date—half the town probably knew I had a crush on him.

Well, I used to, anyway. Funny how fast those feelings fade.

Tentatively, I flexed my muscles, trying to see what I could figure out without moving too much. My arms were tied behind my back. He'd also tied my feet, looping the rope around behind me. I was good and stuck, like a prized calf at the county fair.

Rhythmic breathing sounded nearby, followed by an

occasional smacking sound and a bit of grunting. What was happening?

Then a clod of dirt smacked me in the face. I jerked backward, spitting.

"Oh, good! You're awake." Cliff's feet appeared at the edge of my vision.

I didn't give him the satisfaction of looking up at him. What should I say? Did I tell him what I knew? Would it be better to act confused? Confused, yeah.

"What's going on? I was heading over to see you, and then I can't remember anything. I thought we'd go on a few more dates before you asked to tie me up."

"Nice try," he said. "I know you heard me and Dad talking."

"Talking about what?"

"Stop embarrassing yourself."

"You can't have killed Martha. You were camping," I said.

"Yes, I was. Drove out and set up the site on Monday afternoon, like I told you. Came back early Tuesday morning, parked in the woods, and hiked over. Was back at the campground before lunch. The hardest part was getting out the back of the pool house without anyone seeing me."

Desperately, my eyes went to his hands. "There are no scratches on your hands. She was trying to get away. She definitely got her attacker."

"Ever hear of gloves?" His eyes narrowed. "Wait a minute. How did you know that?"

"I overheard Detective Pratt mention it," I lied. "He thought there might have been a struggle."

"You should have let him handle this. Then you wouldn't be here right now."

A scathing retort sat on the tip of my tongue. Since

annoying the guy who was about to kill me didn't seem wise, I swallowed it. "Listen, there's still time. I know you killed Martha to save your father's business. I know you were only pretending to like me to get access to my house. Detective Pratt knows, too. I called him. If you let me go, he'll go easier on you."

He pulled my phone out of his pocket and shook it under my nose. "Did you? Weird how there's nothing in your call history. I hope you don't mind that I used your face to unlock your phone. You know, there's a feature that requires you to look right at the screen. You should turn that on."

I knew technology was a bad idea! My triumph, however, was short-lived when he continued, "Of course, it won't matter once you join Martha in the afterlife."

"Listen, I get it. You were scared your father might lose his home. I understand. I would do anything to protect the ones I love, too. You made a mistake. I'm sure you feel terrible. I don't have to tell anyone."

"You're not going to tell anyone?" He sighed and shook his head. "You can't think I'm stupid enough to believe that."

"I don't think you're stupid at all."

Talking my way out of this obviously wasn't going to work, so I might as well figure out how to save myself. Unfortunately, my mind was still fuzzy from getting whacked over the head. It felt like the wound was bleeding, but without being able to move my arms, I couldn't know for sure.

"It's a shame that this had to happen," he said as he went back to digging. "I really did like you, you know. You seem like a nice woman. And you're gorgeous."

"Oh, yeah? Great. Let's go steady."

"I understand why you're upset right now, but really, Emma, sarcasm doesn't become you."

"Being a lying murderer doesn't become *you*," I snapped back. It wasn't smart to provoke Cliff, but letting my anger flow helped keep the fear at bay.

Angry with him for killing a woman to make more money. If he had asked for money to pay the property taxes, I would have given it to him, no questions asked. Generosity was my grandfather's legacy. I was angry with myself for being stupid enough to be so busy flirting with a cute guy that I never realized he was a killer. Furious that he thought telling me he liked me made it okay to kill me.

Also scared that I was going to die, and nothing was going to help me. Not my extremely low magic, my talking cat, or my missing ghost. What was the point of having any of those things if none of it could save my life?

Cliff tightened the ropes around my wrists and tugged to test them. The movement chafed my arm, and I winced. Stupid rope.

Under ordinary circumstances, I'd have been delighted that he used ropes instead of handcuffs. Rope was made of thread. I could manipulate thread. Usually.

Argh.

Perhaps this whole mess was the universe's way of telling me not to throw magic around unnecessarily. Dottie would appreciate the lesson. Me? Not so much.

A rustling drew my attention to the bushes. Maybe someone had come to rescue me!

...Or watch me die. Rather than the savior I'd hoped for, Pink emerged from the bushes and trotted toward me.

Tears sprang to my eyes. At least I wouldn't be alone in the end.

I started to thank him for coming, but Pink caught my

eye and shook his head. What was he up to? Although I appreciated his loyalty, attacking Cliff didn't seem likely to help.

My cat didn't spring into action, though. Instead, he came over and lay down beside me. My torso grew warm. Then he purred. The warm spot grew and stretched until I realized—he was restoring my magic. Since I couldn't save myself, my cat saved me.

"I knew you loved me," I whispered.

If Cliff heard me, he didn't have time to respond. I moved in a blur.

My now full-strength magic went into the ropes binding my wrists and politely asked them to loosen. They did. I stifled an excited gasp, careful to hold my wrists far enough apart that Cliff wouldn't see the new slack. Luckily, he was pretty focused on digging my grave.

In hand-to-hand combat, I couldn't beat a construction worker armed with a shovel. In a race, guy who'd grown up on these forest paths held the obvious advantage. If I were going to get out of here alive, I was going to have to use the element of surprise, my wits, and a bit of magic.

With all my might, I shoved my power at Cliff, begging his clothes to yank him away from me, toward the grave.

The magic crashed into him. He yelped. Then he teetered, wheeling his arms in a pointless effort to catch himself. I pulled his shirt with my power, keeping him off balance before slamming him toward the hole a second time.

With a cry, Cliff dropped the shovel and fell to the ground. He landed face first in the shallow depression. Before he could get up, I leaped to my feet, asking the ropes around my wrists to open the rest of the way. With a flick of one hand, I threw my former bonds at Cliff. One wrapped itself around his hands, securing them behind his back. The second circled his legs. Then I asked the two ropes to fuse together, effectively hog-tying him without even a knot to be untied.

"What are you doing? Let me up!" Cliff growled.

"That's not going to happen," I said as I retrieved my phone from where he'd thrown it. Luckily, it appeared to still be working, but there was no reception out here in the woods.

Note to self: see if you can pay to build a cell tower on your property.

"I'm going to tell everyone what you did!"

"Tell them what? You tried to kill me and I, a small woman, physically bested you? Go ahead. People will come from all around to see the legend in the flesh. The mansion will be bursting at the seams. Maybe your father could get some of the overflow business." That was mean, but I couldn't help myself.

He swore at me. I'd been called worse. Still, it was time to go.

Leaning down, I picked up the shovel from where Cliff dropped it, in case he got loose before I returned with the police.

Bending down, I picked up my cat and kissed him on the nose. He sneezed and shook his head. I clutched him to my chest and squeezed. "Thank you, thank you, thank you!"

"This is so undignified."

"How did you find me?" I asked, not caring that Cliff could hear me talking to my cat. Considering I'd used magic to defeat him, the... er, cat was out of the bag.

"Walter came back to the mansion and told me what happened. Personally, I thought you'd be fine on your own but he reminded me that you were weak and mentioned that you didn't even try to use magic before Cliff knocked you out."

I sighed and shook my head. "Yeah, that was dumb. Next time, I will rest and restore myself fully before putting myself in danger after the big spells."

"Good girl. Now put me down." He jumped to the ground.

"If you can restore me like that, why didn't you do it right away?"

"You'll never learn if I do everything for you," he said. "Besides, I didn't know you were going to confront a murderer with only a ghost for back-up."

"Never again," I swore. "Let's go back to Toby's. I'd like to check on him. Then we need to call the police."

"You go," Pink replied. "I'll make sure this guy doesn't go anywhere."

With exaggerated care, my cat lowered himself into the grave, stepped delicately onto Cliff's back, and settled down to take a bath. I allowed myself the briefest chuckle before heading down the path.

EPILOGUE

One week later...

With each whack of the hammer, I felt a bit more serene. Working with your hands really soothed the soul. Especially when you got to hit things.

"You're crooked," Pink said from his spot on the ground.

I turned to look at him, sprawled across the grass on his back, so twisted he appeared to be inside out. "How can you tell?"

"I'm looking at it."

A scathing remark was on the tip of my tongue, but then I looked at the wooden post and realized he was right. My new sign was crooked. After straightening it and giving a few more whacks for good measure, I stepped back to look.

Emma's Home for Lost Souls. It was perfect.

"Souls? You're not expecting more ghosts to move in, are you?" Walter asked. I was getting used to him materializing in and out at will. Or at least, I was getting better at not reacting. "I like being the resident spook."

"Not ghosts, specifically. People have souls," I said.

Pink muttered something that sounded like, "Some of them."

"There are all kinds of lost souls. Josie was lost when she got here. We're going to help her find herself. I was lost until my powers found me." I paused. "But sure, we can help ghosts, too. Everyone is welcome."

"Except murderers," Pink said.

"Except murderers," I agreed, thinking of Cliff. "Hopefully, we've seen enough of those."

"You know, I've been pondering how you helped me resolve that issue with Toby," Walter said.

"Yeah?" If he asked me to drive around and ask other people for a bunch of stuff back, I was going to march straight to my room and find an exorcism spell.

"That wasn't my only piece of unfinished business."

"I didn't think so," I said. "Seemed like a minor thing to be focused on for almost thirty years."

"Well, now that I've had decades stuck in this house to think about it, there are lots of things you could help me with. Like cleaning up my old car and getting it running."

"That car is older than my mother. Do they even still make parts for it?"

"Of course they do! It's a classic. Besides, who are you to talk? Your car doesn't work at all," he retorted.

Since he was right, I ignored that. There hadn't been time to fix my little Corolla in all the bustle of tending to Toby, calling the police on Cliff, getting Josie released from jail, and learning to use my powers properly. But I'd get a new battery as soon as things calmed down. Meanwhile, there was food delivery and Uber and Josie let me use her car when needed.

Speaking of my friend and fellow lost soul, I headed toward the kitchen to see how she was doing. She'd been working for hours, trying to perfect her strawberry rhubarb pie. Although I insisted she didn't need to thank me for finding Martha's killer, she didn't want to feel indebted. I liked pie, so I went with it.

"How are you?" I asked, poking my head through the swinging door. "Is your magic flowing?"

Josie crouched in front of the oven door, peeking in through the window. "In about two minutes, we'll know for sure, but I feel better than I have in ages."

"It smells fantastic."

"That's a good sign. Like I said before, my feelings get into the baking. I've been a total jumble of negative emotions for such a long time now, but I'm finally starting to feel better."

"You're safe here," I said. "Walter and Pink walked me through an extra layer of spells."

"I know, thanks. There is a light at the end of the tunnel." The timer dinged. She opened the oven door and started to reach inside.

"Stop!" I cried, grabbing two oven mitts out of a drawer and offering them to her. "You're going to burn yourself."

"You would burn yourself if you tried this, but I'm fine. My cooking magic gives me increased tolerance to heat." Without taking the oven mitts, she pulled out a golden-brown pie. It smelled like heaven, but the sight made me flinch. "Now it needs to cool."

"Does it really? Can't I magic the temperature down enough to eat it?" I pleaded. Sure, I didn't need her to make pie as a thank you, but no one turned down pie.

"Could a cooking witch? Maybe. Can you?" She snorted.

"No offense taken, in case you were wondering."

With a smile, Josie turned and placed the pie on the counter in front of the window. Then she stiffened.

"What's wrong?"

"Who's that?" she asked, pointing.

A Black teenager on a bicycle was heading up the driveway wearing an overstuffed backpack. His clothes were clean, but very well-broken-in. And that bicycle looked familiar.

Last time I'd seen it, I'd just returned from the general store and put it away.

"I don't know," I said. "But I think he's been storing his bike in our barn. Looks like he's finally ready to introduce himself. He probably needs a place to stay."

She nodded to herself. "Looks hungry. I'll make a sandwich."

While she moved around gathering ingredients, I headed out to the front porch to greet our new arrival. The boy stopped, looking wary.

I pasted on a smile that hopefully looked welcoming. "Hi. I'm Emma. This is my place. Can I help you?"

He stared at me without speaking.

"This place is a bed-and-breakfast," I said, in case he was hungry. "I know you've been sleeping in the barn, but the mansion is a lot more comfortable. It's open to anyone who wants to stay. You can have a room and something to eat every morning."

"Breakfast?" It was the first thing he'd said, so I took his interest as a good sign.

"Every day. If we're nice to Josie, we might also get lunch and dinner. Are you looking for a room?"

"Uh, yeah. But I can't pay. I was talking to the lady at the teen center, and she said to come here. I didn't know what to do."

A friend of mine volunteered at the LGBT+ Teen Center in Albany a few times a month. She knew about my unique venture, and had promised to point some lost souls in my direction.

"Yes, of course. Any friend of Olive's is a friend of mine."

"I don't want any favors," he said.

"A room at Emma's isn't a favor," I said. "I'll put you to work around here. But as long as you help, you can stay."

"Help how?"

"That's up to you," I said. "You can tend the garden or answer phones. You can wash dishes. I hate dishes. Once the kitchen gets up and running for all meals, we could use someone to help serve the meals. You'd get to keep any tips."

He smiled tentatively. "I like plants."

"Terrific." I gestured wildly at the surrounding foliage. "We desperately need a gardener around here. I'm no good at that stuff. What's your name?"

"Terrence. My friends call me T."

"I'm Emma."

"Do your friends call you Em?"

"They haven't, but you can. I like it. M and T. You know, together, that makes us empty."

He snorted at me. "You seem like a nice lady, so I'm gonna give you some advice: don't try to be cool."

"Done."

He put out a fist to seal the deal, and I awkwardly shook it. See above re: really not cool.

"Thanks, Em." He waited a beat, as if trying to decide whether to say anything else. "You got a nice place."

"It's a little chaotic. We're just settling in. But once you get used to everything, I think you're going to like it here."

What happens when a grandfather/granddaughter bonding activity goes terribly wrong?
Find out in RISKY WITCHNESS, Book 2 in the Haunted Haven series.

Available everywhere June 2023

GET A FREE NOVELLA!

Sign up for my newsletter at www.adabell.com and receive *Mystic Treasure*. Just a little gift from me to you.

After a busy winter of murder-solving, Aly can't wait to relax with some family fun at the Shady Grove Annual Treasure Hunt. For twenty-five years, town residents have searched futilely for a chest containing the deed to an abandoned mansion on the edge of town. At this point, Aly's pretty sure the treasure is a myth, but she's always up for Shady Grove shenanigans.

When the Treasure Hunt gets underway, a suspicious new resident throws everything into question. Someone's got a hidden motive for participating, and the town may be in danger. Can Aly solve the mystery to save the day?

MYSTIC TREASURE PREVIEW

Today was the perfect day to win a fortune. I wasn't the only one who thought so: The Shady Grove Town Square hummed with excitement. Fluffy white cumulus clouds peppered the sky. Between the slight breeze and the mercury topping out at seventy degrees, this was the kind of gorgeous summer day that made it worth living through the humidity and thundershowers.

Half the town must have turned out to watch this event. Granted, half the town meant a few thousand people, but still. Town Square was bursting at the seams. Set near the end of Main Street, the largest park in town ran a block down to Second Street, with the other end across the street from City Hall. My three-year-old nephew and I stood under a tree, soaking it all in while we waited for my brother to join us.

Thankfully, Kyle hadn't yet seen the guy making balloon animals. On the corner nearest me, a marching band warmed up their instruments, complete with a bagpipes player. Town residents milled around, visiting the booths that had been set up to feed and entertain us. A huge banner extended across the square, welcoming everyone to the "WALTER SPARROW ANNUAL MEMORIAL TREASURE HUNT".

According to the rumor mill, Walter Sparrow was some eccentric millionaire who died about twenty-five years ago. Instead of leaving his money to a relative or a friend or a local animal shelter, he created this big annual party for everyone to try to win the big prize. No one had managed yet. My best friend Rusty suspected the entire story was a lie, and Walter just wanted to make sure we all talked about him forever after he passed.

Considering the amount of money supposedly on the line, I was surprised there weren't fortune hunters sniffing around all year, but Shady Grove wasn't like other towns. Maybe the same forces that led to unusual happenings kept outsiders away?

Or maybe our town was so tiny that no one outside a fifty-mile radius had heard of Shady Grove or old Walter? That was more likely.

Personally, I suspected Rusty was right. The whole thing sounded like an urban legend. An excuse for a big summer party, but anyone expecting to find treasure would be sorely disappointed. Still, we'd teamed up and gotten ready for action. The practice solving clues should come in handy once Rusty finished getting his PI license.

Tugging my hand, Kyle peered up at me with his big brown eyes and heart-shaped face from beneath his adorably oversized sun hat. "What's a treasure hunt, Aunt Aly?"

I resisted smoothing an errant chestnut curl that was so like mine. "It means Rusty and I are going to follow clues to find a lost item that has been hidden somewhere in the town."

"I find it! What did Rusty lose?" Kyle asked.

I grinned at the spark of excitement in his eyes and smoothed a curl off of his forehead. My nephew had been born with the power to find lost objects, a secret we preferred to keep from the rest of the world as long as possible. Psychic powers ran in our family, but we'd recently learned that some people wanted to exploit what he could do. "Thanks, Little Man, but this game is for adults only. Besides, in a game, it's not fair to use our special abilities to win."

"Cheating?"

"Yes, that's considered cheating."

"Oh. I won't cheat." Kyle stuck out his lower lip. Then his gaze landed on one of the tables below the "WALTER SPARROW MEMORIAL TREASURE HUNT" banner. "Cookie?"

With a laugh, I let him drag me to the table, manned by my friend and the owner of the local coffee shop, Julie Capaldi. A self-described "recovering lawyer," Julie was a blue-eyed blonde who'd moved to Shady Grove a few years ago to take over her aunt's business. She'd set out cookies for sale, but also—and more importantly—iced coffee.

"Hey! Looking forward to the hunt?" she asked when we got within earshot.

"You know it," I said. "Rusty's excited to practice his PI skills. I'm here to stop him from picking the locks of every store on Main Street."

She laughed. "He's going to be a great investigator. I miss having him at the cafe, though."

Until recently, Rusty had worked as the manager at On What Grounds?. After helping me learn to use my powers and solve a murder, my new best friend discovered his true calling. I often considered myself fortunate Julie hadn't banned me from her store when he left. Where would I get my coffee?

Then again, I suspected she had a thing for my brother.

"Hey, kiddo!" she said to Kyle before offering him a cookie. "You planning to hunt treasure today?"

"Aunt Aly said I was cheating."

My face flamed. Maybe she wouldn't understand him? Three-year-olds didn't have the best enunciation, and his mouth was full of cookie. I wasn't sure how much Julie knew, either about Kyle's abilities or mine. She certainly hadn't heard it from me, but small towns didn't have many secrets.

"Cheating? That's no good." She gave me one of those 'kids say the darnedest things' grins.

In response, I gave her the most innocent look I could muster. "We're learning new words this week. Anyway, are you entering?"

"No, I can't."

"Can't?"

She shook her head and laughed. "I did it last year. You're only allowed to enter once."

"That's odd," I said. "Kevin did it last year, too. I thought he wasn't entering because he wanted to spend the day with Kyle."

"That's part of it, I'm sure. But yeah, everyone gets one chance." She shrugged. "People with money are eccentric, right? It's Walter's estate, so he gets to make the rules. I'll send all my good vibes to you and Rusty."

At the mention of my partner, I turned to scan the crowd. With the pre-hunt festivities drawing to an end, Town Square had cleared out somewhat. A lot of people still stood around, but most moved to ring the center, where the hunt would soon begin.

About fifteen feet away, I spotted my friend Tiffaneigh Pratt talking to Brad Stevens. The three of us studied science together at Maloney College. She still didn't want to admit they were dating, but the two of them looked awfully cozy. Their matching bright blue shirts with "WALTER SPARROW HUNTER" on the back told me everything I needed to know about their relationship—and my primary competition. Tiffaneigh hated to lose, and she had some flexible ideas about what constituted fair and legal gameplay.

We'd need to keep an eye on her if we wanted to win.

Mystic Treasure is ONLY available by signing up for my newsletter - visit www.adabell.com to get your copy.

Acknowledgments

First and foremost, thank you to Sarah Biglow for encouraging me to run a Kickstarter campaign to launch this series. It did better than I ever thought it could.

Thank you to all of my backers, but especially to those who exhibited enormous faith in me by purchasing the entire catalog: GhostCat, Kris D'Anci, Michelle and John Redding, Sharon Friedman, Stephanie Thornton, Aylkaraemi, Dana, Erin Ratelle, Wendy Altenhof, Hana Correa, Heidi Kruger, Jamie Dill, Jenn Morris, John Idlor, Kimberly Lloyd, Koni Foster, Lauren Hall, Lynne Freeman, Melody Smith, Michelle L., Myrrdin Starfari, Oliver Gross, Rhel ná DecVandé, Rhonda Peek, Robert Anthony Pritchard, and Stormi Lewis.

Thank you to Thorn Coyle, Anthea Sharp, and everyone in the Kickstarter groups on Facebook. I am so grateful for your generosity with your time and knowledge and hope I can pay it forward adequately.

Haunted Haven Series

Emma thought life was weird before she found out she was a witch. Now she's got some pretty cool powers, a snarky-yet-insightful talking cat, and a fabulous mansion-turned-B&B, complete with ghost. Here is your complete guide to the *Haunted Haven* series.

<u>Unfinished Witchness:</u> Emma is thrilled to come into her legacy: not only has she inherited stacks of money and a mansion, she's got magic! Everything is coming up roses until she finds her new chef dead in the kitchen and her other employee accused of murder. If she can't find the real killer, this haunted haven might never open for business.

<u>Risky Witchness:</u> Now that Emma's bed and breakfast is bustling with business, she decides to treat herself to some R&R at the local fancy spa. But when she discovers that another guest died, Emma becomes the prime suspect.

She'll need the help of his ghost to help find the real killer before they find her.

Open for Witchness: When a friend convinces Emma to investigate the mysteriously closed bar in Shady Grove, she finds a ghostly teetotaler who refuses to leave the premises until their killer is brought to justice. The only way to help Ben avoid losing the entire property is to solve the mystery —but the trail has been cold for decades. Can she solve the case in time for Ben's grand opening?

A SHADY GROVE CHRONOLOGY

E ver since Aly moved to Shady Grove, life has been full of surprises. Here's a list of all of Aly's adventures, in chronological order.

<u>Mystic Pieces:</u> Aly doesn't believe in psychics. Too bad she just had her first vision. Her first instinct is flat-out denial. After all, science and magic don't mix. But when a man is murdered, Aly realizes that she may be able to use her strange new "gifts" to find the culprit. If she can avoid getting herself killed in the process.

<u>The Scry's the Limit</u>: Aly's just starting to get the hang of her psychic gifts when she literally stumbles over her favorite professor's body. She's devastated and determined to get justice. But with several people benefitting from Professor Zimm's death, how will Aly find the real culprit before they find her?

. . .

SIGHT SEERING: AS A PSYCHIC WHO GAINS POWERS FROM antiques, Aly is ecstatic to be invited to an estate sale. It's only after she arrives that she discovers the estate's owner didn't die in her sleep—she was murdered.

MYSTIC TREASURE: ALY AND RUSTY ARE EXCITED TO PARTICIPATE in the annual Walter Sparrow Treasure Hunt. As the event gets underway, they realize that there's more to this event than meets the eye. Someone's got a hidden motive for participating, and the entire town may be in danger.

THIS NOVELLA TAKES PLACE BETWEEN THE FINAL CHAPTERS AND epilogue of *Sight Seering*. *Mystic Treasure* is ONLY available by signing up for my newsletter at www.adabell.com. Thank you for hanging out with me!

SEER TODAY, GONE TOMORROW: JUST WHEN ALY FINALLY identified her sister-in-law's killer, they got away—and they're not alone. To make matters worse, someone powerful has cursed the residents of Shady Grove. Aly's powers vanish. Without her psychic gifts, how will Aly find Katrina's killer and save the pet store?

THE PIE IN THE SCRY: AFTER NEARLY A YEAR, ALY'S GOT A PLAN TO bring Katrina's killer to justice. But before she and Kevin can implement it, she has a vision of someone murdering Tony, the bakery owner. As if that wasn't bad enough—the killer looks exactly like Aly.

· · ·

Mystic Persons: Aly just completed the biggest spell she's ever attempted, with a little help. But the magic came with an unexpected side effect, and now she's got to figure out what happened to the dead man in the upstairs bath before her parents arrive for the holidays.

ABOUT THE AUTHOR

Ada Bell is an award-winning and internationally best-selling author who thought that it would be cool to use a secret identity when writing mysteries. After all, who doesn't want a secret identity? She doesn't remember where the idea for the Shady Grove mysteries started, but she freely admits that Kyle is based on a certain precious toddler in her own life. Ada loves Scooby Doo, superhero movies, STEM heroines, and cake. Mmm, cake.

Find Ada online at www.adabell.com, or get access to sneak peeks, news and more by joining her Facebook group or mailing list.

WRITTEN AS LAURA HEFFERNAN

Retail to Riches Series

A Royal Farce: After years of secretly crushing on her friend Pierre, Lila is thrilled when he proposes they start a fake relationship. For weeks, she finds herself hoping their farce could turn into the real thing—but Pierre's hiding a secret of royal magnitude.

A Royal Pain: When Lila and Pierre arrive in Corchenne to meet her in-laws, she's shocked to discover that her scheming brother has already arrived. Can their marriage survive Caleb's shenanigans and the weight of royal expectations?

The Reality Star Series

America's Next Reality Star: Jen went on a reality show to compete for the $250,000 grand prize. But when she finds herself battling another woman for co-competitor Justin's heart, she finds herself wondering what the true prize is.

Sweet Reality: After a killer competitor threatens her new business, Jen sets sail on a new reality show adventure to save the day. But Ariana's back, and she's determined to end Jen and Justin's relationship once and for all.

Reality Wedding: After retiring from reality TV, Jen receives an offer she can't refuse. The Network wants Jen and Justin to film their wedding to fill an empty time slot—and if they refuse, the Network will get Justin fired.

The Gamer Girls Series

She's Got Game: Gwen's dedicated to becoming the American Board Games Champion, and she never ever mixes gaming with pleasure. But when she meets Cody, trying to resist his charm becomes a losing proposition.

Against the Rules: For years, Holly has harbored a secret crush on her best friend's dad. Nathan is young, he's hot. What's a little harmless flirtation while playing games? But when she discovers that Nathan returns her feelings, Holly may have to choose between two of the most important people in her life.

Make Your Move: Shannon's more interested in designing games and rising to the top at work than dating. She's surprised to find herself falling for her roommate, Tyler. Worse, he's dating her boss's daughter. If she makes her move, Shannon could get fired.

Push and Pole Series

Poll Dancer: A delightfully modern twist on *My Fair Lady*: When a promotional video for her pole-dancing classes goes viral, Mel comes under fire from a local politician running for senate. Desperate to save her studio, Mel decides her only option is to launch her own campaign — and win!

The Accidental Senator: After accidentally finding herself elected state senator, Lana Chen is determined to prove her worth. But when a mistake aids the passage of a bill that's going to put her best friend out of business, Lana has to set things right before it's too late.

Standalone Books

Finding Tranquility: Christa Cooper finds the courage to transition after she nearly loses her life on September 11. Eighteen years later, she's confronted by the wife she left behind: Jess, who discovers that the person she knew as Brett is now Christa. Can they find a future together, despite the past?

Anna's Guide to Getting Even: Anna's perfect life has turned into a string of disasters: After a hurricane destroys her house, her ex publicizes private photos of her — which costs Anna her job and her current boyfriend. And after hitting rock bottom, she decides that revenge is the only way forward...

Friction: Britt's always avoided relationships. Then, weeks before she's set to move away, she meets Colin. To her surprise, she finds herself wanting more.

CPSIA information can be obtained
at www.ICGtesting.com
Printed in the USA
BVHW032321140223
658501BV00004B/97

9 781956 819335